The Silence

The Silence

An Anti-Novel and
Absolutely the Very Last Protocol

Jens Bjørneboe

Translated from the Norwegian by
Esther Greenleaf Mürer

Dufour Editions

First published in the United States of America, 2000
by Dufour Editions Inc., Chester Springs, Pennsylvania 19425

Original title: Stillheten (1973). © Gyldendal Norsk Forlag
© Esther Greenleaf Mürer 2000: English translation
of Jens Bjørneboe: *The Silence*

Publication of this volume has been aided by
a grant from the Norwegian Ministry of Culture.

The Silence is the third volume in a trilogy which
also includes *Moment of Freedom* and *Powderhouse*.

Cover design by James B. Elliott

Cover illustration: Frans Widerberg: Fisker (Fisher), 1989.
90 x 70 cms., oil on canvas. Photographer Thomas Widerberg.
Copyright DACS 2000

Dufour ISBN 0-8023-1333-7

Library of Congress Cataloging-in-Publication Data

Bjørneboe, Jens, 1920-1976.
    [Stillheten. English]
    The silence: an anti-novel and absolutely the very last protocol
/ Jens Bjørneboe; translated from the Norwegian by Esther
Greenleaf Mürer.-- 1st U.S. ed.
        p. cm.
    "The Silence" (1973) is the third volume in the trilogy
informally known as "The history of bestiality" following
"Moment of Freedom" (1966) and "Powderhouse" (1969).
    ISBN 0-8023-1333-7
    I. Mürer, Esther Greenleaf. II. Title.

PT8950.B528 S813 2000
839.8'2374--dc21   00-028334

Printed and bound in the United States of America

Contents

Die Sonne tönt nach alter Weise
In Brudersphären Wettgesang,
Und ihre vorgeschriebne Reise
Vollendet sie mit Donnergang.

(JWG)

Translator's Introduction

The Silence (1973) is the third volume in Jens Bjørneboe's trilogy of experimental novels known informally as "The History of Bestiality," following *Moment of Freedom* (1966) and *Powderhouse* (1969).

The trilogy presents the narrator's extended attempt to grapple with the problem of human evil. In *Moment of Freedom* the narrator was concerned primarily with coming to terms with the atrocities of the twentieth century on a personal level, with trying to achieve a philosophical distance. In *Powderhouse* he steps back and takes a longer historical view, proposing that "the permanent witchhunt" is more or less a constant feature of Western civilization, and breaks out whenever our worldview is threatened by new insights.

In *The Silence* the narrator is trying to achive yet other kinds of distance, both geographical and metaphysical. He is now sojourning in an unnamed country in North Africa:

> In a sense one has to go outside of oneself in order to meet oneself, and perhaps one must go outside Europe to achieve greater clarity in one's picture of the continental sickness. Just as the personal process occurs in the meeting with the environment, so it's likewise probable that one must follow a culture's meeting with other cultures, a continent's meeting with other continents, to get a clear picture of its psychopathology. [20]

The theme is illuminated in many interwoven elements (all of which are previewed in the densely-textured first chapter). The narrator's cultural assumptions are challenged by conversations with various people he meets—not only contemporaries, but also historical figures such as Columbus— and with God. Interspersed are narratives of the destructive exploits of the conquistadors. He adds a microcosmic personal dimension as well.

Chief among the narrator's conversation partners in the present is Ali, a black revolutionary intellectual, in exile from an unnamed country south of the Sahara. In his biography of Bjørneboe, Fredrik Wandrup states that many of Ali's ideas come from Eldridge Cleaver, whom Bjørneboe interviewed when he visited Algeria in 1971. The published interview does not seem to me to bear this out. However, Cleaver's persona—"he whose dwelling-place nobody knew"—does make a shadowy appearance at the end of the third chapter, when the narrator deliver's Ali's briefcase to revolutionary headquarters—the description of which matches that of the Black Panther headquarters in the interview.[1]

Bjørneboe was intensely interested in colonial history at this period. In a 1971 essay, "Literature and Reality," Bjørneboe tells of being powerfully affected by the book *Die Weissen kommen* (The Whites are Coming)—"the first comprehensive history of colonialism," by the German journalist Gert von Paczensky:

> We generally think that we know quite a lot about the whites' advance into other parts of the world, against people of other colors and cultures. We know that the whole thing was one big plundering expedition, one continuous assault and robbery; we know that it involved massacres and mass murders, gold and bloodbaths, rapes, slave-trading and genocide. We know, in short, that it was really, really bad.
>
> And yet we know nothing. What we picture to ourselves about colonialism isn't even the palest shadow

of what colonialism was, or what it to some extent still is. Colonial history is in reality a hundred times worse than what we have been able to imagine . . . so terrible that you blanch with shame once you've delved into it. All this has been systematically suppressed, concealed and falsified.[2]

In *The Silence* Bjørneboe, drawing on his past experience as a teacher in a Waldorf school, recounts the exploits of Cortez and Pizarro in the New World in the style of a epic legend–but with a twist. As Joe Martin puts it, "The recorder of the protocols has not simply recorded, but rather translated history into myth. . . . Cortes becomes an Agamemnon or a dark Odysseus. Mexico becomes a Troy as if from Virgil's point of view, that is, from the inside."[3]

Is it possible to atone for these wrongs? That problem is embodied in the figure of The Nice American (in Norwegian, "Den Snille Amerikaneren"—a play on the Norwegian title of Graham Greene's novel of Vietnam, *The Quiet* [stille] *American*). The Nice American's experiences in Vietnam have led him to make a conscious decision to put his expertise in oil technology at the disposal of a Third World country. Yet this does not suffice to allay his sense of guilt for the atrocities stemming from his own country's cultural sickness. He seeks oblivion in drink, and ultimately courts death at the hands of a band of starving children, in a manner reminiscent of Tennessee Williams' *Suddenly Last Summer*—a play Bjørneboe considered a "sovereign masterpiece." (In a 1962 essay on Williams, Bjørneboe notes that the half-grown, hungry boys in Williams' play "are killing a whole culture, our Western isolated-intellectual world, in a single refined and decadent representative. . . . The image . . . is enhanced by the fact that he himself collaborates in the murder. . . .")[4]

The narrator's encounter with a child prostitute, one of the band of hungry children, sends him into a drinking and sleeping-pill binge similar to those described in *Moment of Freedom*. Here more than anywhere else in his writings,

Bjørneboe—whose alcohol consumption was legendary—
makes incisive literary use of his own experience as an alcoholic, in line with the question posed by the narrator at the
outset: "Is it possible that by dint of investigating one single
person's sickness one can find the diagnosis for the whole culture?" [19] He clearly has Western wealth-addiction in mind
as he speaks of his own condition:

> I know something about alcohol: Drunkenness is
> bound up with the structure and form of the entire per-
> sonality, it's a part of the personality itself. I'm good
> for only two things: to keep my hellish records and to
> drink. . . . If I am to stop drinking, not only must the
> image of my personality be splintered and destroyed,
> my personality itself must be crushed, pulverized. This
> man who can't rest, who knows only hard work or
> drinking like a madman, he must be annihilated. Then
> I must build a new personality, starting at the very bot-
> tom. Who can do that? [168f]

The necessity for individual transformation, and its difficulty, must be borne in mind when considering the theme of
revolution. Bjørneboe insists that transformation must take
place within *both* the individual and society. Otherwise all
revolution will merely breed more injustice, more oppression,
more violence.

Bjørneboe's view of revolution thus includes a metaphysical dimension. He is fond of quoting a phrase of the
Norwegian anarchist Hans Jæger (1854-1910): "Metaphysics
or suicide!" From the beginning to the end of his career
Bjørneboe maintains that to deny the spiritual side of human
nature—as the prevailing forms of both capitalism and socialism are bent on doing—is tantamount to individual and collective suicide. Given the difficulty of discussing spiritual matters in the cultural climate of the time, he tends to approach
them obliquely:

Before we know what a human being is, before we
have a clear and unambiguous *image of man*, we cannot
have any clear goal for our experiments and our struggles to create the right economic, social, political,
and—not least—cultural conditions for human growth
and humanity's evolution.

Until we know what a human is, we won't know
what we want.

But the question of life's meaning and the true
human essence is not considered permissible in our
cultural circle. It is like saying foul words in polite society. It is like doing one's business on the carpet. We
have got used to the fact that our most central, vital
question, about "the meaning of life," is almost
obscene, an indecent question, which no one in possession of his intellectual virginity will be improper
enough to mention. If one asks about meaning and
purpose, one is not a serious person.[5]

The Silence is taken out of the naturalistic plane by such
devices as the narrator's conversations with God (or is it
Satan?), Columbus, and Robespierre; his "memories" from
previous incarnations; and examples of synchronicity such as
those involving his friends the Alessandros, and the ensuing
conversation with Ali [138f].

Regarding the prediction in the book's very first para-
graph, "After the *Third* World War the rest of the globe went
communist; the merchants' empire was broken," we must be
clear that by "communism" Bjørneboe does *not* mean
Leninist Marxism. In a 1971 essay he says:

All genuine philosophy is occupied with the same
problem: living together on earth, "making the earth
habitable," as Brecht says. One could say: "politics"
means finding a way in which one can stand to live
with other people, or reaching an agreement about
sharing the earth's riches in a reasonable way, in broth-

erhood, in freedom and equality.

In a sense all philosophy of significance is an attempt to find a humane and usable form of communism. But that is by no means to say that this true communism is the same as Marxist-Leninist centralism, with its elitist theory, its worship of the party, and its unfreedom, oppression and police terrorism. Quite the contrary: it looks as if the Leninist version has led to the art of making the earth even more uninhabitable than it was before Marx.[6]

A number of critics have commented on Bjørneboe's seeming obliviousness to the likelihood of a nuclear holocaust. For example, one reviewer wrote, "Any talk of world revolution as a 'solution' is simply romantic claptrap, since before that there will inevitably be another world war—which will not leave behind any world to revolutionize."[7]

Bjørneboe does indeed believe that the Great Transformation must be proceeded by a catastrophe which will put an end to the stage we are in now—a stage which Dostoevsky calls "the war of all against all." The catastrophe will entail what Bjørneboe calls—borrowing another phrase from Hans Jæger—"humanity's meeting with itself" (the word rendered as "humanity" [*mennesket*] can also mean "the individual").

The war, the catastrophe, and its aftermath are described allegorically in Bjørneboe's next (and last) novel, *The Sharks*. He says in a 1973 interview,

"I believe that during the crisis man will experience himself and his being as independent of battles for material goods, he will learn so to speak to rise above that. But I don't believe it's going to happen in the near future. I believe it was Goethe who said that humanity's evolution must be planned over a longer space of time than we are used to reckoning with . . . and I think that is right."[8]

The transformation, the revolution, which Bjørneboe is describing is an evolution in humanity's self-knowledge, a spiritual rebirth on a collective scale. "The revolution must become continuous, eternal—it must be new every single day; the revolution must be permanent," he writes in another essay. "Otherwise the society will degenerate and fossilize into centralism. It will no longer grow."[9]

Bjørneboe's apocalyptic vision was already apparent at the beginning of his career. His first book, published in 1951, ends with a long poem, "Before the Solstice: Hans Jæger in Memoriam." Here are the closing stanzas:

> All of us feel the fiercest winter's coming,
> turn up our collars, duck our heads and shiver.
> Now it's November, friends, and we're freezing,
> it will be winter before our time is up!

> And there will be no spring before all is burnt,
> till all is burnt down into black ash
> And fulled and purified in winter's cold!
> Only then will the fire age and the ice age end.

The conclusion of *The Silence* is one of the most quoted passages in all of Bjørneboe's works. The narrator ends his labors with "The History of Bestiality" on a note of cautious hope—not optimism, but the hope which lies on the other side of despair:

> I don't believe that humanity is evil, nor that humanity is good—I believe that a human being is partly evil and partly good. Which side shall be permitted to grow and develop depends on ourselves. On a planet where people have freely chosen to let themselves be burned alive for the sake of truth, the good must have great possibilities. The court sat, the charges were read, the witnesses heard, the evidence presented; humanity was found guilty. I kept the trial records. But I miss one voice in the courtroom: that of the defense.

His plea will be a song of praise—of man the incomprehensible—endlessly evil, endlessly good—all-renewing, all-destroying.

Jens Bjørneboe was still alive when I translated the trilogy; it is now nearly 25 years since his death. Once again I must express my gratitude to the many people who made possible the publication of the entire trilogy in English after all this time. In addition I would like to thank the many Norwegians, and others on both sides of the Atlantic, whose kind interest in my growing Bjørneboe web site has kept my spirits up while the publishers' mills were grinding.

Esther Greenleaf Mürer
March 2000

For more information about Jens Bjørneboe and his work, visit the "Jens Bjørneboe in English" online archive at <http://emurer.home.att.net> or <http://home.att.net/~emurer> A number of the sources cited above appear there in English translation.

NOTES

1. Fredrik Wandrup, *Jens Bjørneboe: Mannen, Myten Kunsten* (Oslo: Gyldendal, 1984), 155. The Cleaver interview was published in *Dagbladet*, 19 April 1971.

2. Jens Bjørneboe, "Litteratur og virkelighet" (Literature and reality). *Politi og anarki* (Oslo: Pax, 1972), 270. Another likely source is the German writer Karlheinz Deschner, who has written numerous books on the negative side of Church history (and who edited a volume of Bjørneboe's essays in German).

3. Joe Martin, *Keeper of the Protocols: Jens Bjørneboe in the Cross-currents of Western Literature* (New York: Peter Lang, 1996), 79.

4. Jens Bjørneboe, "Skogene bak Iguana-natten" (The forests behind *The Night of the Iguana*), *Om Teater* (Oslo: Gyldendal, 1977). For a discussion of Williams' significance for Bjørneboe, see Martin, 106-9.

5. "Metafysikk eller selvmord" (Metaphysics or suicide), unpublished fragment from 1972, included in Tone Bjørneboe's introduction to *Bøker og Mennesker*, Artikler i utvalg ved Aud Gulbransen og Jadwiga Teresa Kvadsheim (Oslo: Gyldendal, 1979), 9-11.

6. "Litteratur og virkelighet" 272f.

7. Carl Fredrik Engelstad, "Jens Bjørneboes Europa-regnskap," *Aftenposten*, 11 December 1973. Quoted in Janet Garton, *Jens Bjørneboe: Prophet Without Honor* (Westport CT: Greenwood Press, 1985), 135.

8. "Katastrofen kommer i 80-årene" (The Catastrophe is coming in the 80s), Interview by Gunne Hammarstrøm in *Verdens Gang*, 1 December 1973. In Håvard Rem , ed., *Samtaler med Jens Bjørneboe* (Oslo: Dreyer, 1987), 189.

9. "Anarkismen—idag?" (Anarchism—Today?) *Politi og Anarki* (Oslo: Pax, 1972), 48. English translation in *Degrees of Freedom* (Philadelphia: Protocol Press, 1998), 10.

Chapter 1

It's not a question of whether we like them or want them. It's not at all a question of what we think of revolutions. They won't ask us what we think of them before they come. They won't bother with common politeness; they'll just come, one revolution after another—which together will constitute the Revolution, the great tidal wave which will rise up and inundate us, a wave of hate and fire and blood. The only thing we could have done would have been to do the revolution's work voluntarily, do it ourselves. The wave would have been less bloody then. But we couldn't bear to do the revolution's work voluntarily, so it will come in its own way. What troubles me is the awful resistance which the U.S. and the Soviet Union will put up in our common death struggle. What I would have liked to say, had it been in any way expressible, would have been: When we've hanged the last Russians by the bowels of the last Americans and then divided up the remaining great powers into small, peaceful communities, the earth will again be inhabitable.

But that's an illusion. Everything must go a different way, the way things have gone so far. One can see it clearly: After the First World War Russia went Communist. After the Second World War half of the rest of Europe plus China, Cuba, and a number of other regions went communist. . . .

Now we'll travel forward in world history, because we can move freely in the future as well as in the past perfect: After the *Third* World War the rest of the globe went communist; the merchants' empire was broken. But the price had become more dreadful than before. What if we had walked that road of our own accord? But we didn't want to; we were simply so hard hit by life's general psychic damage that we preferred the bloodbaths. We chose them, so to speak, quite voluntarily and unanimously.

I saw the proof a few days ago. I went over to the globe and held it up to the light, against the window. And while I looked at it, the red boundaries became more distinct, they swelled up, they spread, they ramified, slowly they flowed out over the whole globe. Then I understood that what I saw wasn't the printer's red ink; it was blood, trickling and running out over the globe—the whole globe was bleeding, and the blood ran from it, dripped from every pore of the wretched, tormented earth—the blood ran in a living pattern over the lands and the sea, and I got blood on the hand which held the globe.

Outside the French window, behind the balcony, lies the great city below me. To the right, the ocean; to the left, behind the city, the mountains. Beyond the mountains, the desert. It's a closed, surveyable world—between the sea and the desert. But behind it lies the land of Chaos, a boiling, seething world without boundaries, a world where anything can happen—and where it will happen, too. The irrevocable will come. This time it will happen. But for the time being I hear only the silence. Only silence remains. Nothing happens. Everything just waits. For something which has never been before, and which no one knows what is. We have no idea what's going to happen—we know only that it's coming. After the silence will come the great transformation.

Over all this—the sea and the mountains and the desert and the cities and the revolution, over everything that we don't know what is—stands the sun. It stands glowing in the heavens and follows its course; only occasionally does it stop and stand still and melt, run across the vault of heaven and down into the sea in heavy drops, or in long luminous stripes. Yes, truly: over it all only the sun remains.

There's something else I think about while walking around this great and sun-scorched city. I can walk for hours and hours—in the old town or around the waterfront, past the recumbent, stinking black bundles of filth and hair, sleeping people who lie wrapped in their long cloaks to use the warmth of the sun to sleep in. They lie everywhere, around corners, on sidewalks. If one of them dies, no passer-by will notice it for several days. Some of these clods of earth are almost alive; they sit motionless, looking alive with one hand stretched out. Of course they may be corpses who just sit there looking alive out of pure spite, to embarrass us who are still living. It's not easy to tell. Nothing is easy to tell. What I think about when I go for these ten-mile walks is something entirely different.

I think about what remains of our used-up time. What becomes of spent and used-up, worn-out time? That eroded, decayed time which we leave behind us like excrement, full of the traces of our own lives? Nothing disappears, nothing can be lost or vanish; at the very worst things can pass into another state—but vanish, no. The question, plain and simple, goes like this: What in hell becomes of our worn-down time? Where is it kept, where is it stored? And how much room does it take? After all, we consume huge quantities of it, so there must be an enormous volume involved. Meanwhile we're always appropriating huge quantities of new time; thus one can also pose the question: Where do we keep getting the daily future which is required for our furious consumption? Where does it come from, what is it, and where does it go? There's something shameful about it, in the same way that there's something shameful in our whole cosmic situation— that we live between the deathly cold of space above us and the deadly fire in the earth's interior beneath us. Above all, there's something scandalous about our unknown origin—in the same way that it's scandalous in bourgeois circles not to know one's earthly genesis. But of course the scandal of our obscure cosmic origin is much greater, because it affects humanity as a whole, and because it has cosmic dimensions. The fact is that the whole human race simply has no parents.

This is the blot on our escutcheon. And thereby humanity has become humanity's problem child. We have become our own patient.

And there's that word again: "patient"!

Maybe I get along so well with doctors (especially psychiatrists) because I know that the world is a hospital, populated with patients. Strictly speaking I've never met anyone who wasn't more or less and to a certain degree demented; somewhere or other everyone has his "missing parts," his paralysis or whatever. On top of that, in this great clinic the doctors are deranged as well. And the more you undertake to cure others' sufferings, to cure them and the world, the more of a maniac you become.

The whole world could be mapped as regions of geographical psychoses—let's call it "colonial psychiatry"—and we could establish that an Eskimo becomes schizophrenic in a different way from a Hindu, a Moslem becomes a screaming paranoid in a different way from a Protestant. I've heard serious psychiatrists claim that only in Christian regions do certain psychoses take the form of what we jocularly call "guilt feelings"—and of course the explanation lies in the fact that our Christian churches have suckled us on guilt and regret and rue. Only Christianity could trick us into a vague general feeling of subjective guilt for all the misery in the world. And with that kind of ballast in our souls we sail off to save the world from its misery. A person from a colonized part of the world develops different symptoms of the same illness. Thus you can map countries and provinces, even cities, from a purely psychiatric point of view. And symptoms can turn into epidemics within whole cultures—into collective lunacy. Someday someone ought to write *The Psychopathology of Europe;* it shouldn't even be an insuperable task. The phenomena are easily visible.

You could write a psychopathology of the ghetto, of the poor, of the rich. You could also write the psychopathology of a profession: of politicians, for example—not to mention record keepers. What we all have in common, though, is that we go crazy gradually, little by little, after life sets its madness on us. So it must be assumed that it's life itself which is pathogenic, it's life which leaves ever greater psychic damage behind it. One doesn't go crazy before one's mother has been impregnated; it's only after conception that the damage begins to appear. So there's simply something about life which we can't stand. And little by little we get sick. What's more, we become deranged in the way which is common and accepted in the time and place in which we're born.

Here it's enough to mention the great and well-known Gallic poet who was encountered in Paris with a live lobster on a leash. He was promenading it pensively and with dignity through the streets of the metropolis, and when he was asked why, rather than walking a dog like most decent people, he had procured a lobster to walk instead, the poet answered without hesitation:

A) It doesn't bark.

B) It knows the mysteries of the deep.

C) It tastes delicious.

The answers fix and characterize his anomaly as being tied to: A) his profession (it doesn't *bark*)—indicating that as a poet he was sensitive to loud and irregular sounds; B) the philosophical school he belonged to (the *mysteries* of the deep)— and, finally, C) his nationality: Frenchman (it *tastes* delicious).

I remember an equally interesting case from my incarnation in Petersburg during the reign of Catherine the Great. The great empress had an even greater heart, not only for Potemkin or for the officers of her guard—but also for others of our hirsute friends. At this time and in this same magnificent capital city there lived an English banker. Today I don't remember what he was called, but it was a negotiable and proper English name. One day this faithful servant of the Empress, this worthy and honorable public miser, was surprised in the middle of counting his rubles by the arrival of the Imperial Police to arrest him. Trembling, he asked what it was all about, and received the surprising but unambiguous answer that he was to be taken away to be *stuffed.* The message gave the banker pause. He felt rather depressed as he was led away. Down at headquarters he inquired again, this time of the highest police officer present. Once more he received the same dispiriting reply: The Empress had personally ordered the stuffing; she had even given the name of the worthy imperial furrier who was to stuff him. Our English banker thereupon sank into melancholy brooding; for one thing, he couldn't remember having performed any act which could have displeased Her Majesty. But hardly anyone likes to be stuffed, and in his despair he resorted to something he didn't readily resort to, namely his checkbook—and by dint of a huge bribe, he managed to get a message sent to the Empress inquiring as to the reason why he had fallen into such cruel disfavor that now his days, much against his will, must end under the taxidermist's shears. The matter was soon cleared up.

As I said, Catherine II had a big heart, and it embraced not only officers of the guard and other regiments, but also a four-legged friend and confidante. This friend and comforter in adversity was the Empress's poodle. It bore an English name, not unlike the banker's. One day it died, the friendly little beast with the small, clever, faithful eyes; and it left its imperious mistress—in the middle of a copulation—dissolved in grief and tears. When the Empress, after a few days of continuous coition, recovered the power of speech, she ordered one of her ministers to see to it that the friend of her heart be stuffed, so that she could always have it before her eyes, even after the beast's eternal life had begun. But the always perfidious fates willed that the minister should have a poor command of English, and the only person whose English name he knew was the aforementioned English banker. So from the minister the order now passed to the executive authority, which went into action down the line and ordered the police to fetch the

banker, while informing the furrier that he should be ready
with scissors and knife and salt and tannic acid for his great
task. The order came from Her Majesty in person, and was a
matter close to her heart which should be taken care of without demur or delay. Nor was there any demur either to the
arrest or to placing the order with the imperial furrier.

As the philosophic reader will have discovered, in this
case the psychopathology lies not with the dog or the
Empress or the banker, but with the more highly-placed executive officials, the lower civil servants, the imperial furrier,
and the police—in the form of the specific Russian obedi-
ence-psychosis. No one will understand Russian history of the
last half century without knowing the story of the courtiers,
the furrier and the banker, and the Queen's poodle. One
could go on like this interminably from a geographic-psychi-
atric viewpoint.

Of course I don't always walk around this city lost in
equally harmless memories.

The other day, for instance, I met Christopher Columbus
on the street, between the big mosque by the fish market and
la Banque National. In his own way he looked strange in the
four-hundred-year-old clothes, and seemed rather worn himself. He was slightly under medium height, but powerfully
built, and didn't look at all like an explorer or an adventurer;
he just looked like an ordinary colonist and exploiter. He was
walking along, faintly wagging his head; he stopped to greet
me, and he seemed immensely old and lonely. I looked at
him and was seized with pity at the sight of his bowed neck
and stooped shoulders. His hair was completely gray.

"You're tired, Columbus," I said. But I knew that the
words weren't mine, I'd seen or heard them somewhere:
"You're tired, Columbus." He shook his head before he
replied.

"You know," he said, "I didn't discover America at all."

"How's that?" I replied.

"You see," he said slowly and sadly, "the Indians had discovered America long before I got there."

Of course I knew that it was a matured Columbus I met—
but I understood him. And I'm tired too. I haven't discovered
any continents worth mentioning either. I'm in the same boat
with Columbus.

Here I just walk through the streets. On the stairs which
lead from the balustrade down to the fish stalls there are small
pissoirs built into the walls, where one can make water with
one's lower half hidden from the curious gaze. But what
struck me was that the public had used every single one of
these small pissoirs to discharge business of a far more serious
and comprehensive character than simply emptying the blad-
der. The flies swarm thick as parasols over these places of
defecation. Right beside one of the pissoirs a black figure lies
sleeping, undisturbed by the flies which collect around his
mouth and eyes. It's all a part of life, and nobody knows for
certain that it's really the devil who created the flies. Maybe
that's just a rumor. Something the Greeks thought up.

But maybe it's true, and maybe it's the devil who created
everything. Only Allah knows. But the fact that life in itself is
pathogenic, that in the long run, so to speak, it's *harmful and
unhealthy to live*, is of course telling.

I walk around a great deal thinking about this, and I think
about how it has two forms of expression—the collective
spiritual damage which affects whole nations and continents,
and the personal psychic damage which the individual incurs
through the meeting with the world around him.

Thus one can pursue—let us say—the origin of the
European psychosis on the one hand, and the genesis of my
own madness on the other.

In many ways it becomes more and more inconceivable
that I was ever a child who, without knowing the least bit
about the world, moved through things great and small and
accepted the madhouse. It's incomprehensible that I went
around not knowing what had happened in the world, but
simply accepted everything, looked upon it as given. And
how long this state lasted is beyond comprehension; perhaps
right up until I was sixteen or seventeen I believed that the

world in its way was good, that it wasn't pathogenic. I must have believed that for quite a long time, and so must have preserved a certain degree of wholeness, even if my meeting with the world had long since laid the foundation for the sickness which burst out in full bloom many years later, after a long and insidious, invisible and subterranean growth.

Is it possible that by dint of investigating one single person's sickness one can find the diagnosis for the whole culture? The point is that in an individual soul the meeting with the environment takes place not in the daylight, but in semi-darkness and the obscure twilight of the mind. The point is not the soul in itself, and even less the surrounding world in itself, but *the meeting between a human mind and the world.* There's nothing else to write protocols about. I've been occupied with this meeting for half a century, and it isn't just Columbus who is tired. It's been very wearing for me, and even if many things are plainer and stand in a somewhat clearer light than before, I know that it will still take many, many years before I come out into the daylight. I must grow much older.

By and large, of course, I'm only a remnant of what I was—half a century old, worn down and mutilated by wind and weather and the things that have happened—rather weatherworn and rusty, decayed and windblown and eroded. In a way I've seen too much, experienced all too many things to be able to put them in order, even if I have hours of something resembling peace and clarity. Still, I utterly refuse to recognize a silence and a calm of spirit which is built on having given up the meeting with the world; I won't accept a peace of mind which consists in the mind's having withdrawn into itself and repudiated Babylon. In the old days, when I was even younger and even dumber than I am today, that's the way I kept my head above water: I turned my back on the land of Chaos, and kept afloat as well as I could. Of course that only works for awhile. Now and then I think of Oliver Goldsmith on his deathbed. When the hour had come, he fell victim to a priest who wanted to know if the dying man had peace of mind:

"Is your mind at ease?" asked the divine.

"No," replied Goldsmith, and died.

In a sense one has to go outside of oneself in order to meet oneself, and perhaps one must go outside Europe to achieve greater clarity in one's picture of the continental sickness. Just as the personal process occurs in the meeting with the environment, so it's likewise probable that one must follow a culture's meeting with other cultures, a continent's meeting with other continents, to get a clear picture of its psychopathology.

How did Europe meet the rest of the world?

And what happened at the same time within Europe?

I wander the streets all through the city. Everybody here speaks a European language, the language of the colonial masters, of the master race, long after the Europeans have been driven from the pastures. How did it go, the meeting between Europe and this continent? The meeting in the visible world was uncommonly profound, but it was even more powerful in the minds of both the slaves and the masters. *There* was the real meeting.

I remember, for example, a beautiful morning in flaming sunshine on the almost tropical sea southwest of India Land, as early as the year fifteen hundred and three. The fifty-year-old—and still unknown—world-conqueror Affonso de Albuquerque stood on the deck of a merchantman and looked forth on the riches of Persia, Arabia, and India. The waves shimmered in the sunshine, Affonso had eaten too much for breakfast, and he was depressed because at his mature age he still hadn't appropriated more of this world's goods than a few hundred tons of gold. Then all at once the thought descended on him: What if he could come back here with the King's commission in his pocket and conquer the decisive geographical points—such as Malacca, which controls the exit to the Strait of Singapara; Hormuz, which rules the Strait of Bussora; and Adem, which lies like a watchdog by the Strait of Mecca? The sunshine glittered on the blue and oil-smooth wave crests, and de Albuquerque's shiny, shit-brown eyes flamed. His face was a deep tan after many weeks' life at sea on the voyage around the Cape of Good Hope—but the thoughts which had gripped him and were now shaking up his Portuguese insides sent waves of pallor over his cheeks. He felt as if the hand of God were grasping him around the heart and lifting him up, so that he became light as air and strong as a youngling despite his age. He danced across the deck and sailed into his oak-furnished cabin where, whistling a Gregorian chant, he quickly opened a bottle of port wine, set out his biggest crystal goblet, his inkwell of chased silver with inlaid stones, along with an eagle quill and his marble horn of blotting sand. He took from the cupboard one of his most flawless parchments, whereupon—after draining half of the noble drink from his motherland's fields—he wrote, in his loveliest and most deliberate hand, his masterpiece of a letter to His Royal Majesty of the Kingdom of Portugal. The letter said that if one were to subdue the three cities of Hormuz, Malacca, and Adem as quickly as possible, then the Kingdom of Portugal would completely control the sea routes to India, and in addition could freely plunder, burn, and sink all Egyptian or Arab ships which carried on trade in the region.

God was with Affonso, and not long afterward (only three years later) he could once again look out over the glittering waves and the endless horizon, this time with the title of *Commandore*. The first enemies he sighted were an Arab fishing fleet manned by heathen fishermen; de Albuquerque swung his sword, fired his cannon, and fell upon the fishermen with all five of his men-o'-war. To the singing of holy hymns the armada's crews drove the fishing boats together and set them afire, preparing a sudden death for the infidels: they were miserably boiled before the eyes of the Portuguese, who thanked God with further hymn singing. It was now clear to all that the Lord was with the Portuguese patriots. Afterwards they attacked the two defenseless cities of Masqat and Sohar, which in turn were plundered and burned. This defensive war having found favor with the Lord, Albuquerque next attacked the fortified and truly great city of Hormuz.

They fought bloodily and long, but in the end Hormuz too could be annexed to Portugal. Now the Portuguese practically had India all to themselves, and they didn't neglect the opportunity.

Gold, precious stones, flying carpets, ornaments, spices, and all the gifts of the world flowed home to the motherland. They ruined both Persia's and India's trade, fixed all prices themselves, and in short, lived out the merchant's dream to the full.

Here we see, in de Albuquerque as well as in the King of Portugal, the meeting between a human mind and the world. From the first moment both their souls were filled unto bursting with the thought of the East's boundless riches and of appropriating them as swiftly as possible. In their mind's eye they saw heaps of pearls, rubies, gold, textiles, carpets, trinkets, and all the things which are good for the human soul. They saw gold in chests, in caravans, in shiploads.

And the Lord God looked upon them with favor and let their hearts' desires become reality: there *were* shiploads, and the King let his grace shine upon Albuquerque, so that he was made viceroy over East India and could end his days literally rolling in gold. And the gold flowed to Portugal and on into Europe.

Strange things happen during a human mind's meeting with the world. Sometimes a mind is destroyed, sometimes it's the world which goes under. But generally it's the soul which loses. When I think of old Columbus, for instance, it's clear that he got tired at the end—and he didn't have much to roll in, either. Maybe that's why I meet him in the streets of this city, especially down by the harbor, where it smells of fish and salt water.

As far as Portugal is concerned, in the long run it was the country's interior which was hardest hit; the stream of gold was pathogenic. The country was psychically damaged by the meeting. It acquired such a furious appetite that it literally gorged itself on colonies; the country ate itself to death, and because of the stream of gold from the colonies it never developed any industry or any form of self-support. Even the clothes for the Negro slaves Portugal had to buy from England. Since then the land has lain fallow, and has only just managed to keep alive by sucking the heart's blood from its last colonies, of course with the support of the rest of Europe—which is now likewise feeling the lack of blood, and which has also suffered psychic damage from the meeting with the world outside its own boundaries.

Of course it's not only Columbus I meet here. Recently, for example, I met my father, who turned out never to have been dead; it was just that, in some way which was just as inexplicable as it was obvious, he'd stayed away for more than thirty years. I've met him many times, and it has always turned out that he'd just been in hiding for a few decades so as later to come back and judge the living and the dead. That's really why he's come back again, and his return utterly paralyzes me with dread—my feet are immobile from fright, my tongue is glued to my palate, and my heart stands still in my breast. I think that most of the paralysis is due to my terror of becoming a child again, of not having put all that behind me. Sometimes it involves my going to school again, to high school, and I have to go there forever to get better grades on all the exams I've ever taken, and which I've never had the least use for; I just have to sit there at an idiot's desk, utterly helpless and without rights, without power of my own for anything. I've been taken back there—by my mother— against my will, and the whole thing is a terrible degradation, a rape without parallel—precisely because it's so meaningless and because I don't have the least use for any more schooling, and besides I've been a teacher for many years and have long since settled into keeping accounts and protocols and am no longer good for anything else whatever—but I just have to keep on going to school against my will, being declared utterly incompetent and without rights.

So it's a different experience and a pleasure to meet Ali. He comes from outside—he's from beyond the desert, from a land where there's a dense, dark-green forest, where people move in the forests at night, where chests and cases are smuggled from the coast to the interior, where long columns of men go through the darkness, men who carry the cases and a thousand other things, who don't speak, who dress differently when they come into the cities they don't own themselves—where they're only good for the very simplest, almost unpaid work, where they're only just tolerated, because they don't own their own cities. But when they're in the city, where the police are always armed, they go around soundlessly and silently in places where the police don't come, and they have letters and small parcels with them— then they disappear into the forest again, and they no longer wear foreign clothes, but go around naked in the dark, which they've known since childhood and do not fear. Things are continually being transported at night in the land Ali comes from, but yet it is very silent in the land. It is the land of silence.

Several days ago I met him down in one of the small fish restaurants near the fish market, and since neither of us is a Moslem, we can drink both wine and anisette as much as we want, and we can sit there till past midnight and laugh and drink and tell each other what we've seen or heard. And outside in the dark stand the children in rags and filth, waiting and waiting for someone to come out of the restaurant with bread for them, which they fight over when you throw it out into the street—preferably rather far, so that you can get away fast while the children have their backs turned trying to get hold of a bit of bread. You can also trick your way past them by throwing some coins far over their heads, so that they run after the money. But they'd rather have bread. Children are very cheap here, and can be sold to Ethiopia, which is a

Christian country having good connections with all parts of the world, but especially with India and Saudi Arabia.

Ali was in a highly mirthful, jocular mood when we said "skaal," and I knew he had a story to tell. And he did, too:

"Haven't you heard?" he said—he was having a hard time swallowing from laughter: "Haven't you heard what happened to . . . ?"

He named a well-known West European diplomat from one of the master races.

"No," I said, "I haven't, but I hope it's something really bad—something simply horrible."

"The same thing happened to him that happened to Lawrence in Turkey."

"Lawrence of Arabia?"

"Exactly."

"And what was that? A lot of things happened to him."

Ali started laughing again. And I saw the picture of the diplomat before me; he was the most formal and immaculate gentleman in all Suburbia's *corps diplomatique*—perfectly tailored, tall and slim, with a narrow, well-formed face. He radiated all the dignity of the state, all its immaculacy and its *Übermensch* status. But he also had a personal integrity, an indescribable inborn patrician dignity, and a deep lack of humor. It was impossible to imagine the man in such an ordinary human situation as, for example, sitting on the toilet.

"I mean what happened to Lawrence when he was taken prisoner by the Turkish commandant. You know that in the Orient since time immemorial they've underscored the conquest of an enemy by mounting him from behind, i.e. reducing him to a woman, treating him like a woman and thereby taking away his manhood and his human dignity. The Turkish commandant wanted to perform this anal deed with Lawrence; but he resisted, and was thereupon turned over to the Turkish soldiers, who first whipped him and then had their sodomitic way with him—that is, Lawrence was abused from behind by the executioners and then, amid great laughter, let go."

"But you're not trying to tell me that something like that has happened to . . . ?"—and at once I understood Ali's laughter; this was the ultimate violation of diplomatic immunity.

"Yes!" Ali went on: "His Eminence was abducted and abused by six or eight natives. They did with him what the men in Sodom wanted to do with the angels."

We both burst out laughing again, and neither of us could stop.

"And now," I said, "since his Excellency has been deflowered by the natives, what happens now? He'll certainly never regain his anal virtue."

"For the time being," gasped Ali, "for the time being his Eminence is in the process of putting his house in order. He's leaving here by the next stagecoach. Because he hasn't just lost his virtue, but also his face. All Suburbia is laughing about it, but above all the incident has made a hit with the natives. He can't show himself on the street without meeting grinning faces. Can you imagine him taking part in diplomatic cocktail parties, toasting his fatherland on its national day? While everybody stands there thinking about how he must have looked lying on his belly with his pants down, being used as a *fille de joie* by a whole band of unshaven brigands? No, he must go in search of other pastures."

"But why did they pick *him*? He doesn't look all that alluring, he's thin and rather old and gray-haired? It doesn't make sense—he's no fifteen-year-old."

"It was a deliberate act. He's the ambassador from the former master race—and it was a conscious act of revenge on the natives' part."

I thought about it, but it was impossible to stop laughing. "Still, it's a splendid way of treating diplomats," I groaned: "All these people in their luxury apartments, with servants and an expense account for anything they want. Even the whiskey they get almost gratis . . . and then an anal rape in the midst of all that magnificence. . . ."

Ali had tears in his eyes from laughing; he could hardly talk anymore.

"Has the case gone to the police?" I asked.

"No, no, no!" he gasped. "But it's come to the ears of the revolutionary government in this country. Such things spread terribly fast. All the ministers are supposed to have practically died laughing. Both the Prime Minister and the Minister of Justice sat there roaring after they heard it."

"Couldn't they get the team to do the same with the American and Russian ambassadors?" I asked. "That would really be impressive. I'm thinking of the valiant American people and the heroic Russian Embassy."

"Then where the hell would this country borrow money from?" replied Ali.

"Do you have the details of the incident itself?"

"Just that they screamed the whole time—the ambassador with pain and rage, the natives with laughter and delight. That's all I know."

I sat there and looked at Ali's hands. They were typical Negro hands, and I've never understood why black and white people have such different hands—especially the fingers. My own hands aren't bad; the skin is brown, they're very broad across the back, and with ordinary, formless fingers. My hands are strong. On the other hand Ali has the kind of hands which only Negroes have: slim, long, and with almost unbelievably slender fingers.

People of Ali's tribe are for the most part very tall and very slender, but with Ali it's only the hands which are like that—thin and delicate. He himself is of medium height and stout. Of course his name isn't Ali. There's not a drop of Arab blood in him, and he's black as printer's ink. He lives here under a false name, and nobody knows what he really does, but every day he gets mail which he readdresses and sends on. He doesn't just rewrite the address, but changes the receiver's name as well.

Ali teaches history at the university—he gets a generous fixed salary from the state. I know that he's at the top of the police wanted list in several countries, but here he's safe, and the government won't extradite him to any other country.

The only thing that could happen to him would be for one of the white police's assassins to ferret him out and manage to kill him. But that's not very probable. Revolutionary history is his academic specialty, and he's well covered by his profession as a university instructor.

We ate fried shrimp, which we cleaned with our fingers while the oily sauce dripped from them. Then we washed them down with white wine, and afterwards we ate mandarin oranges in brandy. Finally the coal-black coffee. Our joviality lasted throughout, because the picture of the flawless and elegant ambassador and his sexual degradation was unforgettable.

"How's it going with your comparative revolutionary history?" I said.

"*Merci.* I'm working on the history of the twenty-first century."

"You're studying the revolutions of the future?"

"It's a fully coherent chain. In the 1700s people were dealing with the first truly revolutionary century. It brought the great revolution. In the nineteenth century things went further; the revolutions became international, they spread from country to country—just think of 1848 or 1871. But only in the twentieth century did revolutions occur which were carried through—even if there have been many abortive starts. In any case, we've seen revolutions carried through: let's say in Russia, in Cuba, in China, in Yugoslavia, in Albania—and add to these, for example, the country we now happen to be sojourning in—along with all the revolutionary states in those geographical regions which you, with unsurpassed impudence and arrogance, call "the Third World." Despite the fact that India and China had had several thousand years of history before Europe even came into the picture, you really say "the Third World"—you regard Europe as "the first." But the line through the centuries is clear: the eighteenth—revolutions; the nineteenth—more revolutions; the twentieth—the first wholly successful revolutions over great parts of the world; and then the twenty-first—where the consequences are drawn and the world revolution is carried out. In the next century we'll enter a completely new phase of world history—then the entire globe will be socialist."

"When will the revolution be complete?"

"Probably after the middle of the twenty-first century."

"Do you think, Ali, that it's right for you Africans, Asians, and Americans to take your revolutionary theory straight from the Europe you hate? From the Europe which has plundered and sucked dry the entire colonial world? You get your whole theory from a German Jew and petit bourgeois, Marx—and from a Russian lawyer of bourgeois origin, Lenin. And I'm saying 'German' and 'Russian' with everything that entails. Is it really true that first you must have Europeans to suck you dry, and then you need Europe in order to straighten things out? Can't you save yourselves?"

"Listen," said Ali: "You Europeans are completely out of it. You still think that Marx and Lenin are the same today as they were fifty years ago. Only in Europe do people discuss the pure, orthodox doctrine. We from America or Asia or Africa—we don't have the European obedience in our blood. We've been obedient to the master races a little too long— and we've learned our lesson. To us Marx and Lenin mean entirely different things than to you, because we've understood what's central in them, and we don't go around repeating dogmas learned by heart. We *know* that they're Europeans, and that they must be carefully adapted in every single corner of the earth. When Western Europe ends up being the last part of the world to complete the revolution, that will be because the Europeans to this very day interpret them literally—not a tittle of the doctrine must be changed. *We* change everything, and we take what we can use."

The warm winter night outside the restaurant was full of children. They were black-haired but light-skinned, the way people are here. And when anyone left the place, the minors gathered around them in a howling swarm. The beggar flock would force the guests up against the wall until they brought out the bread they had with them and threw it over the children's heads and into the darkness beyond. The hungry flock would run for dear life after the bread crumbs, and would fight over them, tearing them out of each other's hands and mouths.

One of the girls was big; she was around twelve and probably sexually mature, as you could see through the thin dress which was all she had on. This was striking, since even very poor parents in this country don't usually let the girls stay out in the evening after dark. She had a thin, light-brown face and dark, curly hair. She was hungry, and one could probably do what one wanted with her for a few kroner.

The fish restaurants look out on the harbor, and are dug in under the boulevards so that they seem like caves or tunnels under the city. Innermost in each cave is the kitchen, and the opening of the cave is a glass wall facing the street. Since the day had been mild despite the time of year, the windows had been taken out and a number of tables and chairs were set out on the sidewalk under a heavy awning. Right beyond the awning the children hung out.

I sat looking out at them.

"Soon that'll be the only thing we have to offer tourists in this country," said Ali. "People come here from Europe and America, and they're disappointed that it isn't exotic and picturesque here anymore. The only thing which consoles them is the hungry youngsters, who make them feel that they're in Africa. They give them small change instead of bread, and when the youngsters get home—if they have any such place—the money is taken away from them. The bread they eat here."

Outside, the flock of children grew and came closer. The children got bolder; a couple of them came almost all the way up to one of the outer tables before a waiter chased them away. Some began to screech. They formed a dense wall beyond the sidewalk, and their unrest grew. All at once a wild yell came from the flock, and the children pounced on something which had fallen into the filthy gutter. There was a brief wild scuffle, after which things quieted down again. Then my eye fell on an elderly man in a fez, but otherwise in European clothes. He was sitting at one of the outside tables and had broken his portion of bread into small pieces, which now lay before him on the table, and which he was throwing to the children one by one. It was as if he were sitting in the Piazza San Marco feeding the pigeons. Now and then he would fool them by pretending to throw a bit of bread, but actually keeping it in his hand. He was harmlessly amused by the confusion which arose when none of the children could see where the bread had landed. Then the waiter brought his fish soup, and he buried himself in the meal and the rosé, both of which he obviously found tasty. The youngsters stood for a long time waiting for more bread, but the game was over now. He sat hunched with the bulky napkin knotted around his neck, plucking shrimps and pieces of *scampi* out of the rich soup. Nothing in the surroundings could disturb him any longer. The bits of bread he now rolled into little balls, which he dipped in the soup before eating them.

"You've seen enough," continued Ali; "you don't need to see any more. You know all you need to know. For example, you know very well that what remains for us is just as much a psychiatric task as a political one. The sum of all colonial history is that both parties have been spiritually damaged by the meeting—both the colonial peoples and the colonial masters are sick from the events of the last few centuries. The natives have gone though so many humiliations that at bottom, even in countries which are now free, they regard themselves as third-class human beings—or even as some kind of apes who have learned to dress in European clothes and speak the masters' language. They've learned to drive cars and to despise themselves. And the master races have been damaged because they've gotten used to treating people as if they were animals; and now—when the slaves have risen up and cast the masters out—the master races don't believe their own eyes, because it all runs completely contrary to their own theories. They stand there watching the slave peoples taking over their houses and their offices, but they can't quite believe that it's real. They can't imagine that the native apes can keep trams and buses going—or that the airports still function.

They see and they understand that the natives are mentally ill in a different way than they themselves are, but they don't understand that the one madness is just as good as the other. Basically—and this was most evident during the war—it was a shock for the master race to see that the natives could become deranged in an ordinary human manner; you might say that it was a kind of proof that they were human, and to show that a native had an ordinary nervous breakdown or genuine paranoia was terrifying to the white doctors. It was as if they thought: If the natives really have the potential for becoming schizophrenic just like us humans, then there will soon be no limits to what the blacks can think up. Even the European image of sickness they were conceited enough to want to keep for themselves. In fact, they assumed that the natives were too dumb to be able to adorn themselves with anything so fine as a serious neurosis or a real psychosis. They simply didn't think that an African could have enough soul to get sick. But now after the war it has turned out that we have more than enough of it to be able to get the same sicknesses."

"It's not true," I said, "that mental illnesses are necessarily proof that one is human. In my part of the world, for example, they're very common among animals, especially among dogs. One of my friends has a great Dane, a bitch who is an old maid. She's never wanted to know any male except her master, who is human. So one day the old maid got pregnant. She got milk in her breasts and her belly grew. Finally the owner took her to the vet, who found that the dog wasn't really going to have puppies, it was a hysterical pregnancy. And the strange thing was that the pregnancy was brought to term. The puppies came into the world, even if they were invisible to everyone but the mother, who lay there licking them and giving them milk all day long. Gradually the puppies got bigger and began to crawl around on the floor, which created terrible difficulties, because only the mother could see where they were, and an outsider could very easily have the bad luck to step on them. Then the old maid in the basket would begin to growl and show her teeth, so that you'd immediately have to

move. The dog's owners got used to it and learned to avoid
stepping on the puppies; but if they had company, things got
difficult. Furthermore, I know a cat who was paranoid. It
thought that it was continually being persecuted. But neither
the bitch nor the cat became human because they had human
illnesses. Both the cat and the old *virgo intacta* were wholly
qualified for years of psychoanalytic treatment. So you've by
no means proved that Africans are people. That smidgeon of
mental illness you're bragging about is no more than what pets
have where I come from."

Ali smiled.

"Have I told you," he asked softly, "that the Belgians used
to cut the hands off those of us who weren't industrious
enough? Sometimes they did it to put terror into the
populace—to show who the masters were, who had the
power. They did it to children, too. When I was young I saw
people who had had one or both hands chopped off.
Sometimes they did it just for amusement. I know of a man
who had his right hand lopped off when he was six years old.
Naturally one can ask oneself who ended up the craziest—the
colonial masters or the natives who were continually in mortal dread of them. It's also possible that the dread was
mutual—but so long as the whites were superior in weapons
technology, they could defend themselves. Still, the terror of
what can happen, once the natives are strong enough, always
lies there underneath the brutality. They figure that the blacks
will treat them as they deserve, if they get strong enough.
After several centuries of terror neither side is normal anymore—neither the executioners nor the victims."

"Ali, how can you slander the Europeans like that? You
have them to thank for everything. You who'd never seen a
pair of trousers before you were twenty—but simply dressed
in the very cheapest palm leaves. . . ."

"I went to the mission school as a young boy. By the age
of nine I knew that it was a sin to commit adultery, and that
Jesus was a product of the most scientific virgin birth. The
Trinity I was also familiar with. I knew, too, that all superi-

ors and higher-ups were installed by the Lord of Sabaoth—
and that my obedience to them was the same as obedience to
God. Since the whites were the superiors and higher-ups, it
was the duty of all blacks to obey them. In addition, of
course, we were whipped and mutilated whenever it pleased
Jesus and the Virgin Mary or the Holy Ghost. In general we
were whipped at every opportunity, which was necessary in
order to make human beings out of us. My father was
whipped several times, really whipped so that the blood
spurted and the urine flowed. All this was necessary in order
to get us to work—as you know, the blacks are lazy, they
don't like to work without pay. They had trouble understanding that they must sacrifice themselves for the motherland which protected them, and in general were much more
inclined to hope that someone would protect them against the
motherland. Where the chiefs were concerned, whipping was
a specialty, and so that their chieftainly dignity shouldn't go
to their heads, it was common—and certainly necessary as
well—to force them to drink the urine of the master race's
officers—of course with the rest of the tribe driven together to
watch. It was a practice which gave a convincing impression
of the motherland's motherliness and strength. He who loves
his niggers lets them drink his urine."

"And you can sit there and say that," I said, "without giving a thought to all the high culture and humane civilization
which we've brought you from Europe. I'll mention not just
Christianity and banking and firearms, but also trousers, col-
lars and syphilis. So it's true what they say: you blacks can't
feel gratitude—you simply can't say thank you. The same is
supposed to be the case in India: people can't say thank you
there either. You never think about how we've brought you
Martin Luther and Albert Schweitzer and built millions of
schools and billions of hospitals, where you can go and get
pills for your damned syphilis, just as if you were our own
children—ignorant and ungrateful, but still beloved children.
We'd hardly discovered America—where the Indians had
lived for thousands of years without being discovered—

before we took you along to the West Indies, Brazil and
North America. I still have some of the prices in my head,
and it's a shame how much was paid for some of you. I'll only
mention some of the few figures I remember by heart. And
they're in hard currency, in divine, celestial American dollars.
It wasn't uncommon to pay up to $1200 or $1250 for a sound
and healthy nigger, preferably one who'd had chicken pox
and other childhood diseases and had gotten over them. Up
to 1250 dollars! Who do you think would have paid anything
like that for a worn-out black here in Africa? And yet you
can't say thank you. Especially nice and strong and skilled
blacks might go for even more. Over there you became
Christian and inherited eternal life. And those who stayed
behind here in black Africa, they became Moslems for the
most part, so after they died they had to journey down to the
kingdom of death and stay there and be roasted for all eter-
nity. You're exactly like the English say the Indians are: you
simply can't say thank you. Can you think of an uglier quality
than ingratitude, Ali?"

"No," said Ali; "it's terrible. The part about lopping off our
hands, and sometimes our feet as well, went along to America.
Of course it became especially fashionable with disobedient
slaves; as for those who they thought might run away, they
simply chopped their feet in half. They'd chop off the foot in
the middle of the instep, and dip the stump in boiling oil to
stop the bleeding. After awhile the nigger in question could
resume his work, even if he'd acquired a rather delightful way
of walking. But he couldn't run away. There's no doubt that
the Europeans have brought us culture and civilization."

"Yes," I said; "just think of the Bible schools. Where
would you have been without them?"

"We would have been lost!"

"My people up at the North Pole have done a lot for you,
too," I went on: "They've collected money for the missionaries—and for generations, so to speak, they've sat up there by
the howling North Atlantic in snowstorms and winter darkness, knitting both woollen socks and woollen mittens for you

and your black brothers in Madagascar and God and the devil know where. Besides, we pray for you. To God. So He'll forgive you and look upon you with mercy, even if you are ungrateful."

"I want some more wine," said Ali and looked around for a waiter.

"Is it good for you?" I said. "It takes less than that to make you disobedient and obstinate. Wine and Negroes—they hardly go together."

Ali turned and waved, and one of the waiters slowly walked over to us. He was a thin, middle-aged little man with a black mustache. He smiled.

"Ali wants some palm wine!" I said. "Will you bring him a gourdful?"

The Arab grinned with his whole face:

"Don't you want to make it a keg right off?" he said.

"No, just an ordinary calabash of fermented coconut milk."

"I'll have a bottle of ordinary red," said Ali.

"What would you have been without the colonial masters' vineyards?" I said.

"Our vineyards are the country's misfortune," replied the waiter: "It's made the whole country specialized. We can't live on drinking wine; we must convert our whole production to make it more diversified. We didn't produce any wine before the Europeans came here, and only after the oppression began was our agriculture converted to the monoculture of wine. The French forced us over into this one-sidedness after 1830."

"It's strange," said Ali: "I'm thinking that this was in fact in the middle of the July Revolution in France. Do you remember Delacroix's picture of Freedom leading the people at the barricades? There you have one of the symptoms of Europe's sickness: revolution at home and colonization abroad. One could go all the way through history drawing such parallels between what was happening simultaneously in Europe and in the colonies. In 1830 the workers, students and bourgeoisie go to the barricades—the king flees to England, Delacroix paints the people fighting in the streets, the bourgeoisie assume power again, create a new king, France conquers this country and crushes all resistance, Delacroix paints exotic Arabs and luscious harems, and the plundering begins in earnest. Achmed, how were things in this country before 1830?"

"The country had it very good," replied the waiter: "We had two universities and schools everywhere, even in the smallest villages. Practically everyone could read and write."

"That's right," said Ali: "But a hundred forty years later we have in this country over ninety percent illiteracy."

"Our own language was forbidden," replied Achmed. "Only the conquerors' language was allowed in the schools and in the administration—and our own schools had to be run in secret."

"What happened with the next revolution, in Paris in 1848?" I said.

"France had just made Tahiti into a protectorate. The U.S. won the war against Mexico. France forced Abd-el-Kadar to surrender." Ali counted quickly on his fingers: "War against the Kaffirs in South Africa. England conquers the Sikhs. The rulers win on all fronts. The domestic revolutions are put down and foreign peoples are subjugated."

"When was this country conquered?" I asked.

"According to the conquerors' calendar, in the Year of Our Lord 1454—that's when the Pope declared that the African West Coast should forever be Portuguese territory."

"That's remarkable," I said. "*Quattrocento* has always been a fascinating time. Now I'm speaking as an old Tuscan. At the same time that you blacks became Portuguese, Europe's culture was founded in Tuscany. I'm thinking not only of the fine arts, but also of science. There's nothing in modern Europe which doesn't come from Tuscany."

"Yes," said Ali: "The gold. The wealth comes from us."

"No," I said; "the exploitation of the tenant farmers, the serfs and the propertlyless also bore fruit. It wasn't only the colonies which were sucked dry; Europe too was colonized.

But somewhere one must get the gold and the wealth which is the prerequisite for creating a new culture. The leopard is a beautiful animal, but it has to eat other animals to be able to grow and develop. It costs money to build a cathedral. And without a small group of people who are excused from a life of production, there wouldn't even be so much as a single bust left from the whole fifteenth century."

"In the succeeding centuries, Europe's enormous wealth came from Asia, Africa and the colonies in America."

"It had to be like that," I replied; "you can't create a culture by a show of kindheartedness. You need gold. And you don't make a revolution by feeling sorry for people, or by writing radical poetry. You make a revolution with guns and not with theater pieces."

Then Achmed came with the bottle, and after that he got one for me too. This conversation never ends; every time Ali and I meet, it continues.

"Ask Achmed how you make a revolution," said Ali. "He knows."

"Achmed, do you make a revolution with poetry and plays or with weapons?"

Achmed thought about it while I looked at his thin, yellowish face with the little black mustache and the missing upper teeth. His waiter's outfit was a towel which he had tied around his waist to protect his pants and shirt.

"Nobody makes a revolution," he said. "The revolution comes when people can't stand any more, then it arises of itself—but then you need a few leaders who can guide it. Otherwise it won't be a revolution, but an unsuccessful rebellion."

Achmed was in a nerve clinic for almost the whole last year of the revolution because of the maltreatment he'd been subjected to as a prisoner of the Europeans—for awhile he was in the same ward as two of the executioners. But he seems well now. At any rate he does his job as a waiter very well. The only thing is that he never remembers to bring the check, but assumes on principle that all bills are always paid.

Chapter 1

When you've finished eating, Achmed always goes out on the street and over to the nearest bar and gets some black coffee, which you're served as a gift from the restaurant. That you aren't allowed to pay for.

We talked for while longer, while Ali and I sat drinking wine, with Achmed standing beside us. When the hour was past midnight, we got up and left.

As soon as we got out into the darkness, the howling flock of children was upon us. They yelled and screeched like lunatics, danced in front of us and held out their hands for bread or coins. They seemed somewhat different now, probably because they were tired and should have gone to sleep long since, if the hope of some bits of bread hadn't kept them watching outside the restaurant door. I had bread with me and broke it up into rather large pieces. Then I threw a couple of pieces over their heads and into the darkness. They disappeared after the bread, and it was a few seconds before they were back again. They returned with a fury even wilder than before. They screamed like crazy and the yells must have been audible far up in the city, which was growing quite still now. Once again I threw bread to them, and now we managed to get away, while they themselves went back to the door to wait for the very last guests who were still sitting inside.

"Don't you ever give them anything?" I said to Ali.

"I'm not a tourist," he replied.

A moment afterwards we heard a new yell from the children, and we knew that the door had opened and a new guest had left the restaurant.

Ali's car was parked up on the Boulevard Che Guevara, and an old beggar stood beside it, looking after it. Ali gave him a coin, and the man bade Allah bless us, then sat down and drew his cloak over his head. Ali drove me home, out to Suburbia outside the city itself.

Only when I got out onto the balcony did I discover that there was a full moon. And I sat in the basket chair and looked down on the city lying below me in a silver veil of moonlight. The night air was still mild.

Now and then I think about my own life, but more about
people I've met and about countries and cities I've seen.
Sometimes I think about particular animals I've met, and
about how they're faring now. I thought about a dog I'd had
when I was quite small. Even when I'm lying on my
deathbed and am perhaps a very old man, I'll probably
remember this dog. Not because it was exceptional, but
because it was mine. It's remarkable that of all things the
image and memory of a little dog which lived almost half a
century ago can still go on living in the consciousness of a
man who has seen and seen and seen so much of the world
and so many people. The picture of the little dog is alive in
me now, as I sit here on the veranda in the moonlight with
such a foreign city below me. This little dog is one of the
things I remember best of all. In one corner of the dining
room there was a cupboard, but it wasn't built for a corner, so
behind this cupboard there was a triangular space, into which
I would sometimes crawl and hide when I wanted to be
alone. I could sit perfectly still in there and think my own
thoughts for a long while at a time, and often the little dog
would come in to see me. It also turned out that it sometimes
went there alone, but then it was on another errand. It did its
business there, but in an unusual way: it would put its stern
against the wall, and then move sideways while it emptied
itself. It was as if someone had taken a tube of toothpaste or
shoe polish and squeezed it out against the wall, while moving the tube over toward the corner. When the dog had done
its business, it left behind long stripes at rump height on the
wall. Maybe in its way it was a rather exceptional dog after
all. But I didn't think about that. This little dog I remember.

Probably Ali also has such things which he remembers
from his childhood and his country. He certainly must have,
and someday I'll talk with him about it, and not just about
revolutions and colonies. But the way it's been so far is that if
I ask Ali about his childhood, he just tells about his father
who was whipped several times and about his uncle whom
they killed with a stick inside the prison.

I sat there long enough to see the moon glide a good way across the sky while I was sitting there. I also remembered my bicycle very well, because it was from abroad and looked different from the bicycles the others had. It was a little lighter too, and I'd taken off both the fenders and the brakes, so that it became even lighter, and one could ride faster on it. I must have been unusually absent-minded and dreamy as a child, because I collided with cars three times, and was quite badly hurt—even with so few cars as there were in those days.

I can't understand why these childhood memories make me so terribly sad. After all, I've survived both childhood and youth, and now I get along pretty well in my way. At any rate so long as no one bothers me. I can manage my own affairs and keep accounts and records, and nobody has power over me any more. But I can't understand how I can sit here so far away from my childhood and my country and have everything so clear inside me—how I can take this with me wherever I go, and always, always have these pictures to think about. I can't understand why it all must eternally go with me, all this which is imprinted in the spent and used-up, worn-down time. The time is gone, but not what happened—that can never disappear, it goes on living inside me, it goes on existing.

It's a long time ago, and at the same time it has just happened. Besides, it's not so bad as long as one has something to laugh at. So it really shouldn't be anything to get upset about. The whole thing is dreamland, anyway. But I can't grasp that we have consciousness—and a consciousness which encompasses so much; it spans world history and my own life, but this little private enterprise of a life fills my consciousness just as much as world history does. Of course the question is how my own little excrement of a life is related to world history— in other words, it's a question of a relationship: *Does a single existence function within the contemporary part of history?*

Far worse than remembering one's childhood is recalling one's youth. It must have been much more painful than I realized. If I merely think of friends from the earliest period of youth, I involuntarily clench my teeth and close my eyes, as when something hurts physically. I don't think it's bad conscience—for I wasn't any meaner to them than they were to me. The shabbiness was mutual. No, it isn't bad conscience or shame! I only know that to remember is to relive—and I don't want to relive anything whatsoever. Not a second. I've used it, eaten it up, I'm done with it. I have no past. It lies somewhere in the common store of worn-out, worn-down, worn-thin, threadbare, leprous, and misused time. But it doesn't belong to me any more. It's simply a part of humanity's enormous store of infamy, something that is done by humankind to humankind, and which no longer concerns me at all; it isn't my property.

I often dream that I'm on the moon. In general I doubt that many people dream so much about the moon as I do. Last night, for example, I was on the moon again. But it's an entirely different moon from the American one—not even to mention the Soviet one. For instance, one can go to church on my moon, and there are big trees growing there, both stone pines and trees which only look like stone pines, and huge firs and terebinths—all the trees there are a bit terebinthlike, and now and then it snows, but then the snow melts and only remains in big patches around the stone pines and all the churches. The first time I was on the moon and saw what it was really like up there, I was unutterably happy to see that it didn't look at all the way people think it does. And this thing about there not being any atmosphere, that's slander, malicious gossip. In reality it's very nice on the moon. It's the only place where I go to church.

For a long while I sat on the veranda and looked at the moon. And I knew that my childhood was no longer mine, and everything felt better. Then I got up, drank one more large glass of wine, and went to bed.

I no longer go to sleep in the same way as before—by degrees and little by little, so that one slowly glides over into thoughts and pictures which then dissolve. Today I go to sleep as if the blood suddenly left my brain; I feel wool inside

my head, like wadding or cotton-wool, and I notice that I'm
fainting. Then it's hardly more than a few seconds before I'm
sound asleep.

First I lay there for a bit and thought about Ali and his
childhood, which he doesn't want to talk about—and then my
thoughts glided over to the Land of Silence where he
belonged, to forests and the dark streets in the cities where
the master race lived, where something was happening in the
forests all the time, where something was being done, something was being prepared—under cover of the forest, under
cover of the darkness which is black like his brothers, and
which will aid Ali when he returns home to help cast out the
foreigners who have been there and ruled for almost five hundred years. In Ali's land there are two groups working
together to drive out the rulers; one of them is just nationalist,
and the other—to which Ali belongs—is also revolutionary.
When together they've thrown out the whites, then they will
turn on each other, and those who are the strongest will execute the others' leaders—so that after the fight for liberation,
either Ali himself will be executed, or he will execute others
of his countrymen. It can't be otherwise. But until then there's
only one thing which counts—and that's the men in the forest, the cases they carry, the stores of high explosives and
guns, until then it's only the darkness and the forest and the
black men who count. And over it all, over the forest and the
darkness and the cities, stands the moon. I remember that
fourteen days ago it was as thin as a sickle, and lay flat on its
back, the way it does down south here . . . but already before
the moon is new again, much will have happened behind the
silence in the forests in Ali's land.

On the Art of
Making the Earth Uninhabitable

Of course I'm a European. I know this part of the earth, and
it is my world. But something has gone wrong with it.

And it's Europe's own fault; no one can say that the continent wasn't warned, or that *we* weren't warned. The warning
cries have been strong enough down the centuries, but no
one—or at any rate very few—heeded them. It has been a
thankless task to be a prophet of doom in this valley; on principle Europe has chosen the false prophets every time she
had a chance.

For this reason Europe today has a long and painful history of illness, a history of preferring lies to truth, gold to
human kindness, power to understanding. We've preferred
the disease to the medicine. And we've exulted over our false,
bloated, sick health, we've prayed to the Caesars and we've
cried "give us Barabbas" for two thousand years. We've eaten
with the murderers and scorned the victims. And we don't
even have the excuse that we didn't know better. We've
always known of other possibilities, we've had an almost free
choice between understanding and violence—and in the history of our own sickness our choices stand like milestones:
gallows, stakes, and crosses.

When did it begin?

The sickness goes back more than two millennia. Suppose

we look at Alexander the "Great"—the ruler who had the
doctor crucified when his own darling little boy died of fever
despite that same doctor's treatment. The deification of such a
figure as Alexander already shows what was sick in Europe;
and with this philosophy of shit we've spoon-fed innocent
youth on our continent through the centuries, generation after
generation, down to the French and American torturers who
in our own time have been tyrannizing the rest of the world.
And that isn't all; to new generations we've represented the
river of blood which followed the Europeans' trail through
other continents as trivial beside all the heroism and the over-
flow of humane and Christian spirit shown by the executioners. To this every good European can naturally rejoin: Were
the others any better?

And the answer falls in three parts: A) Yes, they were better. . . . B) Let others sweep in front of their own doors; I
sweep in front of *mine*. . . . C) It's a poor excuse for our own
bestiality to ask whether "the others" weren't just as greedy,
cowardly, and brutal.

Add to this the hypocrisy and the lies about our "heroes,"
about Albuquerque, about Stanley, about Clive and Hastings
and Cecil Rhodes and the whole murdering band, whoever
they are.

In the year 1600 Giordano Bruno was burned alive. It was
a good year in general; at the same time the English founded
the English East India Company. Europe was rapidly moving
forward. There followed, as on a conveyor belt, the estab-
lishment of the Dutch and the French East India Companies.
But these were fruits of a successful previous century.
Precisely in the year 1500, Brazil was "discovered" by the
Portuguese Alvares Cabral—and simultaneously, back in the
homeland, they saw what the blacks in West Africa could be
used for: they discovered that, as with all other things of this
world, they could also trade in niggers.

As early as 1364, shortly after the "Jacquerie" peasant
revolt had been quelled in the homeland, French traders
sailed along the coast of Guinea and visited the land above

the mouth of the Senegal. The great peasant rebellion is put down in Germany, with Martin Luther's enthusiastic blessing, and the plundering spreads from continent to continent.

The sight of others' land and wealth becomes a covetous obsession, a European rabies, a thirst for gold which obliterates all humanity and decency in the powerful. With the Church's blessing, raid follows raid. The meeting with the other continents develops into an orgy of blood and gold, the blood flows down into the homely earth in Asia, Africa, and America—and the gold streams to Europe. At the same time all disquiet is suppressed back home in the "motherlands." For centuries the madness rages, and Europe gets used to the idea that all the earth's wealth belongs to us as a matter of course. Defending one's property, one's life, one's land, one's children's lives, is regarded by the whites in the colonies as mutiny and rebellion; the whites send "punitive expeditions" and exterminate whole populations who have proved obstinate. Everywhere the knee must bend and the head bow to the intruders. Still the "rebels" don't surrender. In the 1770's the American colonists revolt against England, in 1789 the French Revolution breaks out in earnest, two years later the blacks of San Domingo rise against France. The world is still divided in two, into masters and servants, but it's creaking at the joints.

The murderers, muggers, and thieves appoint themselves "the motherland," and it's a strange motherliness they show to their black, brown, yellow, and red children. Never has the world seen such mother love. Never has it seen more bloodthirsty mothers. Everywhere there's more gold to be looted, the pillaging goes on and on, hand in hand with the oppression of the legitimate children back home in Europe—and the curious thing is that it's the same circles of power which are involved in both cases. The power and the wealth are gathered into steadily fewer hands. Thine is the kingdom, Amen.

There's something called settling your accounts—putting your house in order. You have to pack your bags. And the strange thing is that to settle Europe's account is to settle one's own. I pack my bags at the same time that Europe's history of spiritual sickness becomes clear and intelligible to me. For it's all blood of my blood, flesh of my flesh. To dissect Europe is to cut up oneself, because it's one's own thoughts and instincts and passions one meets in the stinking, cancerous intestines one finds inside the freak, inside the monstrosity. This stinking mixture of blood and sickness is my own interior. But I shall continue to cut myself up, continue to dig around in inflammation, pus, and purulence—until we've seen all the entrails of this pretty picture. Until we see where the rabies has led us. Love of others' gold, indifference to others' blood—these are the chief symptoms.

It's just a matter of following the trail of blood.

I meet Ali fairly often, and it strikes me again and again how little hatred he and his friends bear. It scares me—it really frightens me, and it gives me the feeling that they must have hidden the hate somewhere—you might say put it aside in order to keep it in reserve—so that it can someday be let loose and drown out all other words and thoughts. I have a feeling that one day they'll kill me, they'll cut me up in pieces, throw me into the sewer. But that's my own feeling, and there's nothing in Ali, or for example in the waiter Achmed, to give me grounds for suspecting it. It's just the lack of visible hatred which makes me so uncomfortable.

"You all talk so much about your own Hitler, but to us there's nothing special about Adolf Hitler. It's just that Hitler tried to do the same thing within Europe that the whites to this very day are doing outside it. For us there's nothing new in that. A couple of technical angles may be new—let's say the gas chambers, the tempo and precision of the genocides— but these variants are actually more humane than those employed by the whites in the colored parts of the world. We're used to it, and it doesn't faze us. We're not the least bit shocked by Hitlerism—it's just an introverted version of the usual white modus operandi."

Ali has said this to me often enough that I know he means it. And I've asked him:

"Then Hitlerism is just an extension of ourselves, just a manifestation of our own insides—you might say Europe's first real meeting with itself? Is Hitler Europe's soul?"

"I don't understand why you all take Hitler so seriously," he replied. "He's a rainy day. He's nothing special. The racist ideology and the master-race idea aren't Hitler's invention—very single French or English or Dutch colonial corporal whom Our Lord created has lived by the same ideas as the fascists. But to them it was such a matter of course that they didn't need to give speeches or write books about it. I really don't understand what you all get so excited about! It's instructive for you to be treated, for once, the way you've been treating others for centuries. You ought to be grateful to Hitler: at least you've learned something from him—or at any rate *could* have learned something from him."

During one of my walks through the metropolis, while I was strolling along thinking how strange it was to be outside Europe and the white man's domains altogether, I met Columbus again. We met down by the harbor, where we both feel at home because of the smell of sea and fish and boats. He was just as always, in his worn, ancient clothes, stoop-shouldered, his face freckled by the tropical sun. We greeted each other as usual, and exchanged a few words about the wind and the weather. Then he said:

"Has it occurred to you that it was I who brought syphilis to Europe?"

"It was just as much your crew who did that," I replied.

He heaved a sigh and passed a hand over his forehead:

"Lord, what a bunch that was! *That* crew! Think of coming to a strange continent and having only people like that with you—murderers and robbers and crooks—pack of thieves, the lot of them. Has anybody thought what a burden it was for *me* to have such a band of shits along, such a gang of bums and looters?"

"Those who came later were no better, Columbus. Your crew were bandits and thugs, all right, but so were all the others."

He ruminated in silence for awhile, mournfully stroking his chin and shaking his head.

"They were a dreadful pack of swine," he said softly. "That was no ship's crew I had along, it was just a herd of pigs, and gold and lust was all they had in their heads."

"They were true representatives of Europe," I said. "There's a deep and many-layered symbol in the fact that you arrived in America with such typical Europeans on board."

"Do you think so?" he rejoined slowly and thoughtfully: "Do you think so?"

"Of course, Columbus—history doesn't play with coincidence."

"It helps to hear that," he replied after a pause. "For what must the Indians have thought of us! After all, I didn't choose this stinking swinish flock of murderers voluntarily—you know that the king and queen. . . ."

"*Everybody knows that, Columbus.* Today every school child learns that you didn't pick out your gang of shits yourself."

"Are you sure?" He raised his head and sent me a friendly look of relief: "Do people really know that today—everywhere, I mean? Have the Indians heard about it too?"

"Everybody," I said, "everybody."

"That makes me feel better," he said, and nodded the way old people do: "because you can't imagine how they behaved. They stole and plundered and manhandled and raped. They were insatiable in their thirst for gold and sex. But, since you've said it yourself, those who came after me and this murdering band of mine were no better, even if they had higher titles and commissions. They burned the Indians over a slow fire to get out of them where they had more gold. That's the way they were."

He was silent again for awhile, then he sighed and looked at me with his old seaman's eyes.

"I should never have gone," he said. "That voyage

brought nothing but misfortune and misery. I should never have set out—but I was young and didn't know what it would lead to. America should never have been discovered."

"Nobody could know that," I said, and laid a consoling hand on the age-bowed shoulder. "Besides, I can tell you something I haven't wanted to say before. It wasn't you who were the first European in America. It was some countrymen of mine, they got there long before you did. They sailed across the North Atlantic, straight over from my country. You know where I come from."

"Yes," he said and nodded, "from Sweden."

"Not Sweden, it's. . . ."

"Oh yes—it's Iceland, then." He looked at me searchingly: "And it was really your people who came first . . . before me?"

"Yes," I said, "the misfortune had already occurred. The leader was named Leif Erikssønn, and he discovered the United States back before the year 1000. That was 300 years before Marco Polo returned from China, and five centuries before you landed on the islands."

"Never heard of him," said Columbus slowly. "So it's only the syphilis I have the credit for."

"Leif Erikssønn called the land Vinland and took a few Indians back with him as prisoners. Later many people headed west; but then America went out of fashion, and nobody sailed there anymore."

"Had I known that," he said, "had I known that . . . then others could have taken care of the syphilis."

"Don't worry about it," I said; "syphilis made itself useful in Europe. It became our communal disease, and acquired— like every beloved child—many names. Syphilis became the soul of our people."

"What do you mean by that?"

"Haven't you heard how many prominent men died of lues?"

"Not a thing—?"

"They were really the best of us. They were poets, prophets, artists, and philosophers, inventors, scientists . . . the whole intelligentsia—naturally with a number of lesser lights as well: kings, statesmen, generals—and in addition, of course, lots of rank-and-file soldiers and seamen. The latter, especially, saw to the geographical spread of the disease; and the fact that today it's so tremendously widespread in Africa is due both to our officers and to our missionaries. To Asia, too, syph was brought by our best men and empire builders."

"That must have been after my time," replied Columbus.

"Many researchers are of the opinion that for some individuals syphilis can entail a brief but enormous increase in their intellectual and creative powers. As examples I need only name Nietzsche and Hugo Wolf or Maupassant, Heine and Baudelaire, Beethoven and. . . ."

"Who the devil are they?" he said, looking at me in confusion. Then he shook his head: "So many things happen, so terribly many things. . . ."

"At any rate, you don't need to be ashamed of the syphilis you brought us."

"So it came to mean something for Europe?"

"*Something?* Almost everything! It began with your sailors coming back to Spain. . . ."

"They were no more 'sailors' than I am a camel!"

"Well, anyway, that so-called crew of yours came home and went ashore to wives and whores and everything that moved on two legs. With the utmost devotion to their great task they sowed syphilis all over Spain, with a conscientiousness and a thoroughness which is still seeking its historical counterpart. Not one province escaped."

"Go on."

"The next phase was to spread the fruit of the meeting with America as fast and as far as possible, so that it might do its work—permeate the blood and marrow of men of action and creativity, take root as an inflammation and fever in the nerves and brains of the elect—driving them to superhuman achievements in mastering the world and in creating works of art of unsurpassed power and beauty. As you remember, it was in the month of March 1493 that you returned to Spain after your first American expedition—to the port city of Palos, where eight months earlier you and your band of freed criminals had weighed anchor to find the sea route to India and prove that the earth is round like an apple as it sails about the cosmos. So you came back one morning in March—the same year that the Spaniards conquered Grenada and drove out the Moors, and the Pope fixed the boundaries between the Portuguese and Spanish colonies."

"Yes," he replied, looking out over the sea before him: "It was a March day, with a stiff breeze on the port quarter. We sailed out with three ships, but only two returned. The people were gathered in great crowds by the harbor and yelled and yelled with joy. Then I sailed up to Seville. . . ."

He nodded placidly at the pictures before him which only he saw and recognized.

"Almost all of us had little sores on our sex organs while we were over there on the islands, but in the course of the homeward journey our rashes and eczema had mostly gone away of their own accord."

"It's quite true that you started spreading it in Seville—and then followed the stay in Barcelona, where all the heroes were shown the generosity which heroes need. And now the small tumors and sores began to spread at a furious rate. The inoculation was accomplished. Syphilis now went its victorious way to Naples, where the Spanish troops supported the Italians against the French siege in 1495. In their distress the besieged hit upon the brilliant idea of sending all the infected women out of the city and over to the French enemy, who gladly took their Italian sisters under their care and treated them with the greatest brotherliness. Soon the whole French army was well impregnated, and when the Frenchmen turned their faces toward home, syph had all of luxuriant, beautiful Europe at its feet. The victory march became a triumphal procession to the interior and northward. Soon Europe was one big hospital."

"Fancy that!" said Columbus, smiling and nodding faintly: "So it went via Naples—through my own beloved Italian homeland. Yes, yes."

"And quick as lightning all of Europe became syphilized, via France to Germany, Germany to Poland, and thence to Russia. And all levels of the population—from beggars and vagabonds to kings, emperors, popes, and cardinals—got to share the blessing from the islands you had visited. But what's even more impressive is how fast the Europeans managed to export the great itch on to India, China, Africa, and the whole world. That was the price the rest of humanity had to pay for the American gold which now filled Europe's coffers."

"Yes, yes," he answered resignedly, "that part of the story I know. But in America, how did things go over there? The same misery?"

"Yes, Columbus. Blood and gold, nothing but blood and gold . . . and so it has gone on. The Indians were slaughtered and the Negroes brought in, and it was the same old story . . . down to this very day: blood and gold and blood and gold. . . ."

"So at least it's good that they named the continent after Amerigo and not after me."

He sat there for a long time without speaking, then he said slowly and faintly:

"You know, sometimes I long for the sea again, to feel a stiff wind and to have the honest planks of a deck under my feet again . . . to feel the rhythm of the waves and the silence … the silence. . . ."

"Yes," I said. "At any rate you knew the dream, the adventure, the longing for infinity, expanse, the wide open spaces. One of our Nordic poets has written some verse about you. Part of it goes:

> There is no God in the raging waves;
> There you will find the heart of Columbus
> Who created a new world
> Out of his earthly torment."
> Columbus raised his head and looked at me:

"Dreams. Adventure. I don't know what you're talking about. Longing. No. I don't know anything but scurvy and syphilis. And if I had any heart, it lay not in the waves, but in the coffers in Spain. What I dreamed of was gold and power—like all the others. It was the gold which drove us, every last one of us. . . ."

"Excuse me," I said, "but you were the one who said that you longed for the sea, for an honest ship's plank under your feet."

"Yes, yes, yes—but that's today. I wasn't like that back then. We didn't set out from longing or love of adventure . . . but after gold. To become governors or viceroys, or at least to get into the administration, quite simply to get a decent job in an office."

"You're tired, Columbus."

"Yes," he answered and nodded. For awhile he sat perfectly still, sunken into himself. Then he nodded again.

"Terribly tired," he said.

"What about the story of the egg—the egg of Columbus?" I asked.

"Hogwash. Pure invention."

It sometimes happens, when I'm walking through this great city, that I once again long for Europe. I may long for the altar at Isenheim or the Palazzo Vecchio, for Chartres and the Tower of London. I long for everything which is my own interior, which formed all the pictures I had inside me when I was young—and which I thought was the world. And for the landscapes, for the west coast of Jutland, for the Cinque Terre coast north of Portovenere. For the Arctic coast and Mont-Saint-Michel and the rocks on the Atlantic coast of Brittany. And it's a strange pain to break out of all this which was once truth for me, and which gradually became a cage of prejudices and compulsions. Were I to put it in the classical manner, in the style of the great tradition, then I'd have to say: A European isn't something you are, it's something you become. And you become one only when you settle your account with Europe, which is simultaneously an account with yourself—that is, the reckoning with the prejudices and with the terrible burden of guilt which clings to this continent, and which we ourselves participate in right up until we see that this burden of guilt is our own, and that it lies not so much in our actions as in our whole way of thinking, and in our enormous ability to choose wrong. I almost said: To choose *Evil.*

I was talking with Ali about Europe; and Achmed, as he does so often, was standing beside us and smiling.

"*Pardon,*" said Achmed, "but tell me how things really are in your own country. What's happening up there?"

"Everything's just fine, thanks," I said; "the population loses its teeth and the vegetables wither. In the lakes the trout drift around with their bellies in the air, and along the riverbanks the salmon float ashore with open mouths. In short: *trade and industry are flourishing.* We've always lived on war profits, and thanks to continual wars in the Middle East we're living high on you—a few years ago the shipping industry achieved a profitability which far surpassed the bull markets during the First World War."

"So it's really going splendidly!" replied Achmed seriously.

I went on: "There's money, sunshine, and progress on all fronts. Taxes are rising, but only for the poor. Overuse Inc., the Exploitation Co., Fjord-Pollution Ltd., and the Mercury & Prussic Acid Corp. between them control almost the whole country, in close collaboration with Wiretapping Inc. and such enterprises as Eurosulfur and Euronapalm. In the shipping industry we have in particular Global Graverobbing Inc. Agriculture has been taken over by Bankrupt Estates Ltd.; the fisheries are controlled by the Church's Emergency Fund. The Garbage & Refuse Corp. looks after the cultural life. As you see, Achmed, we've come pretty far for such a small country. Confess that you admire us?"

Achmed didn't smile, but because Allah has made him a waiter, he filled our wine glasses. "Yes," replied Ali, "we really admire you. We've even copied your idiotic European clothes. You've managed to make the earth uninhabitable to a degree one wouldn't have thought possible. By dint of your

precocious weapons technology you've succeeded in destroying the social structures and economic foundations in Africa
as well as Asia and America. You've squeezed gold and
wealth out of the colonies, and you're still doing it. You've
transformed paradise into hell—and for that we're actually
insane enough to go on admiring you. The madness goes so
far that today a great many politicians in the former colonial
possessions want to imitate the European form of society—in
other words, to copy the economic system which has made
the earth uninhabitable. We admire the bandits who've seized
other continents'—*our*—riches for themselves, and who've
used these riches to destroy the world. All of it—wars, geno-
cide, exploitation, and now, finally, the pollution of air, earth,
and sea—it all has the same cause. And this we admire. But
you can be sure that some of us understand this—and that we
won't end up building a copy of Europe after the wars of
liberation are over."

"Listen," I said, "how are you going to create a new society with all the age-old compulsions you lug around? I need
only mention the way women are viewed in the Arab countries. We can take one of the psychiatric examples from the
war—a case which is internationally famous, in fact. It concerns patient X, an active saboteur, guerrilla, and freedom
fighter. While he's in the resistance he finds out that the
European military police have abused, tortured, and raped
his wife. A while later he breaks down, he becomes wildly
depressed and, above all, impotent. His wife writes to him
that she is dishonored; that he mustn't think of her anymore,
just forget her. Now to everybody around him the man is the
main person, they're only concerned with him and his fate.
The wife is simply regarded as a spoiled and rotten piece of
fruit which can be thrown out. On the other hand, everybody
finds it quite natural that the man, as a free guerrilla soldier,
should go after other women; the trouble is just that now he
can't make it. He's totally impotent. He becomes the object of
everybody's sympathy and concern—and no one would have
regarded him as dishonored if he'd been able to make love to

the women he went after. The wife—who was raped—she is lost and dishonored. And she herself shares everybody's view of the matter: she regards herself as ruined for life, a disgrace to her husband and her family. Now the husband, the patient, says to the psychiatrist almost these very words: 'If they'd just maltreated and tortured her, *that wouldn't have done anything to me*. But who can forget something like this?' See? It wouldn't have done anything to *me*! And everybody else has the same attitude: it's the *husband* they're sorry for. The most macabre thing is that even the doctor obviously takes the same view: it's the *husband* who is dishonored by the rape. Nobody gives a damn what happens to the wife. Do you think, Ali, that this shows a view of humankind and society which is better than the European one?"

"What you're saying," he replied, "just shows that you whites are completely incapable of understanding anything about the Africans. The case is entirely different from what you see. Back of it all lie thousands of years of fine, invisible threads and unspoken thoughts. For this man the whole world has collapsed, and both of them—both he and his wife—have been marked by it for life, and for both of them what's happened is wholly irreparable. It affects not only themselves, but both of their families and also the children they already had together. No African would have difficulty understanding this, but you whites just project yourselves into what you're investigating—and you don't grasp anything of what lives inside the Africans. You think that if the natives here just learn to speak a European language and wear European clothes, then they're like you—only dumber. And with this attitude the Europeans have raped, tortured, and murdered for centuries in this part of the world. These are the reasons why Africa today is one big incurable, bleeding wound. With gun butts, bayonets, and soldiers' boots you've trampled and manhandled human bodies all over the continent—but you don't know that you've trampled and battered human souls even more. What you've done here will never dawn on you.

"You're like that in everything that has to do with politics.

I don't know of anything so comical and so helpless as the sight of Europeans sitting and studying Marx; he gets memorized, dogmatized, interpreted, and expounded. The Russians are probably the worst. Of course they're also great chess players, eminent logicians—but their way of thinking is just as rectangular as the chessboard and its squares.

"And this European or 'white' logic functions splendidly in all mechanical relations, in everything which has to do with mechanics and technology, with machine-building and physics—but in respect to human beings it's a total failure. And politics is an art or a science which has to do with human souls, with human fates. And here the logic of the chessboard doesn't help any more. You see the results in history. And perhaps you see it most plainly of all in our own century, because it bears the fruits of the past.

"Look at the map of Africa: it isn't divided up exactly like a chessboard, but according to the same principle; Africa's boundaries were drawn up at desks with a ruler, after conferences between military chiefs of staff. Not the slightest attention was paid to tribal boundaries, to peoples or to nations, but only to degrees of latitude and square kilometers. It will take centuries for us to recover from the damage done by this slide-rule logic. No tribal chief in the interior of Africa would have been capable of thinking in such a foolish way as the mathematical geniuses on the general staffs of Europe."

"So you think that in the year 2000 the Afro-Asiatic and Latin American Cultural Research Commission will declare Europe and North America to be mentally underdeveloped regions and send us foreign aid?"

"I think that man was not created for the Sabbath, the Sabbath was created for man."

"And what does that mean?"

"That man was not created for socialism, but socialism for man. It's that simple. That means that our task is not to produce the new Soviet-African man, but an African socialism—a socialism which can be used by Africans."

"At least you admit that Europe has produced socialism?"

"Are you crazy?" Ali retorted. "We had socialistic and communistic tribal societies in Africa long before anyone else thought of it. Our old tribal democracy was one of the most painful obstacles to the colonial powers—a fact which they usually expressed by claiming that the chiefs didn't have enough authority. If we were dissatisfied with a chief, he was simply deposed, something the Europeans could never conceive of because they were brought up on the idea of a centralized, absolute state power—which the Europeans still believe in. Of course the Europeans have produced a socialist theory for socialized industry, but they haven't made it a reality. In the socialist states of Europe they've merely produced a caricature and a bugaboo of socialism, a ghost which for fifty years has stood in the way of a true socialism. That's due to the peculiarity in European thinking—the need to rebuild society into a chessboard; and when the whole thing goes wrong, they begin making up fables about the future 'socialist soviet man,' a kind of abstract dream figure who will fit into the chessboard, but who has never existed and who never will exist. When man—that is: when reality doesn't fit the plan, then you think that it's reality which has something wrong with it; you can't imagine that it's the plan which doesn't fit the reality.

"Just take the flock of children which stands outside here in the evening, shrieking and begging. In a European country they'd have the police round up the children and commit them to a children's home, to get the youngsters off the streets. They would have removed the visible symptom that something in this country isn't as it should be—but they wouldn't have touched the disease which causes the symptoms. And they would have driven around the streets with garbage trucks to gather up the poor who lie sleeping on the street like heaps of rags, so that the streets would be clean and pretty to look at—but they wouldn't have abolished the reason for the misery. You don't solve any problems by shutting the beggars up in state poorhouses—especially not when the poor themselves prefer sleeping on the street to being committed."

"Europeans would think that the commitment was for their own good."

"Europe has never understood anything but violence," he replied.

According to what pious men have brought to light by deep and profound study, it pleased God to let the noble Spanish hidalgo Hernando Cortez see the light of day on the same date as Martin Luther—the fourteenth day of November, the eleventh month in the year of Our Lord 1483. The one was to further God's Protestant kingdom on earth, the other—the young knight Hernando—was to spread the true Catholic doctrine throughout the Aztecs' ancient heathen realm, from sea to sea. One became a burner of witches, stout and fond of good food; the other, a mighty slayer of infidel Indians and a collector of gold, pearls, and other treasures—for Spain and for himself. And the spirit of the Lord descended upon Hernando Cortez, so that already as a child he pricked up his ears when he heard the world "gold." At the age of seventeen he cut short his legal career, for he thought that more gold was to be got in that part of India to which poor old Christobal Columbo had found his way, than here in this already rather worn and shabby Europe. And while don Christobal wasted away from pain and sorrow in impoverished circumstances (at least for a great admiral), the young hidalgo journeyed to the New World, arm in arm with his gilt-edged fate. He didn't waste any time.

In a most distinctive way the One who holds the starry heaven, the sun, and the fixed stars in his grasp had blessed Don Hernando Cortez with the blood of a carnivore. He was a European to the tip of his penis. Cortez junior would have let his mother be roasted alive over a slow fire if it would bring him two gold florins. He was an ornament to his country and the pride of his church.

With such men a country can rule the world.

Ah, there's an abyss between Columbus and Cortez!
But Columbus had a son.

In contrast to his father and in common with Hernando, he knew where there was gold to be got. The two geniuses settled in the West Indies. For those who don't know the reflections of the sun, the mad light on the foam and the waves of the Caribbean Sea, the words may not say very much. That's possible. But the sea is gold and white foam and sunshine and sunshine and sun and sun and a sky which is blue and orange, and all is light and gold and light and gold, and at the bottom of the sea, far below, lie mussels with pearls and pearls and pearls—with sharks and giant squid and poisonous sea urchins—but all is gold and pearls, gold and pearls.

Yet the whole Caribbean world was only a slum, a poor farm, compared to that which was later to be discovered, and which Cortez would come to harvest: Mexico.

At length, yet while he was still very young, Cortez had laid up a considerable fortune, even for a colonizer—first by trading in slaves and importing Indians from the Lucayo Islands to the island of Hispaniola (where the natives were already dead of slavery and too much forced labor), and then by taking part in the conquest of Cuba. Then something entirely new happened in his life—the very thing he had been awaiting forever: he received a great kingdom to plunder. It is here that his heroic saga begins. He found his fortune in Cuba, whence he set forth to make all the nations his victims.

Thus does our God stand by the bold.

The islands in the Caribbean Sea were plundered rather swiftly, and the population exterminated at an impressive tempo. An astonishing number perished just from the forced labor, whipping, and disciplinary punishments imposed by the whites. Order was kept until soon no more were left to keep order among. A goodly part of the population was likewise dispatched by torture and the stake in an effort to force hidden treasures out of them. Another excellent method of dispatch was pearl fishing, in which the slightly-built Indians were forced to stay underwater the whole day from sunrise to sunset, bringing up mussels to the Christians. After doing such work for a certain length of time the redskins fell sick; they developed hemorrhages and diarrhea along with severe rashes, and, on top of it all, red hair as well. Finally they were buried. Strangely enough, the same thing happened with the natives in Brazil, to which Alvarez had found his way at the turn of the century. And this singularly high mortality led to something totally new: the importation of black slaves from Africa to the New World. And this is momentous, for one day a Negro was put ashore on the North American continent. He was just an ordinary Negro, but he came to be of inestimable value to Cortez: the black brought chicken pox with him to Mexico—a disease which was harmless to the whites, but deadly to the Aztecs. In their struggles to take land and property from the Mexicans, chicken pox proved to be a great help to the Christians. It was clear to Cortez that God had sent the disease into the land to aid him, now as often before. And doubtless it was so.

This Negro of the chicken pox was the first black the Aztecs saw, and also the last.

In the course of thirty years the native population was reduced from twenty-five million to six million. How this ideal result was achieved, Cortez's story shows us. It can be taken as a model by all who wish to follow in the master's footsteps.

On the islands the natives were gentle and simple-hearted; therefore they had little wealth or gold, and let themselves be exterminated to the last child, as it were, without taking it amiss. How different was the population which Cortez and his brave men met in Mexico! Already at the coast, in the small towns, they met *Indios* with gold ornaments and precious stones of overwhelming beauty and numbers. Many were clad in capes of woven gold, with headdresses of gold and pearls and rubies; but unhappily the Mexicans had weapons as well, and often seemed resistant and combative. Still, it's putting it mildly to say that Cortez's mouth watered at the sight of the country's worldly goods. It came to his ears that far inside the continent lay the great city of Mexico, where dwelt the ruler of the whole country, the emperor Montezuma. Montezuma was the mightiest emperor in the world, and his treasures and riches were without equal.

Of course the Aztecs, despite their exceedingly high culture, had no firearms—a circumstance which Cortez did not fail to appreciate. And he decided forthwith to subjugate Mexico for the Spanish crown and to take from the Emperor and the people every single precious stone and every grain of gold they might possess. To be able to do this with good conscience and with full right, Cortez went ashore with men and priests and, in his most sonorous Castilian, read aloud the following proclamation, fabricated by Spanish scholars for the use of the Godfearing on similar occasions—namely, whenever one was taking possession of others' land and, in accordance with the Christian faith, declaring it to be Spanish property, so that all disobedience would be rebellion against the crown and against God's kingdom on earth:

"I, Hernando Cortez, servant of the most high, most mighty kings of Castille and Leone, civilizer of barbaric tribes, message-bringer and *Capitano*, do hereby declare and proclaim to you that all the nations of the earth have been given by the Lord our God into the keeping of one man, whose name is St. Peter, and into that of his earthly successor, the Holy Father in Rome, the Pope, lord of Christendom and of all the world, who in turn has vested their Catholic Majesties, the Kings of Castille, with the right of ownership of all islands and continents on this side of the ocean. . . ."

When Cortez had further made it clear to the Indians of the village that every disobedience against Castille's deputy, Hernando Cortez, would thus be rebellion and treason against God and the King, and hence could not be punished harshly enough, he concluded the proclamation of his assumption of power as follows:

". . . . If you do not submit, then will I—with the help of God Almighty—lay you under the yoke of Church and King

with might and main and compel you to obedience; and I shall take your wives and children and make them into slaves, and I shall cause you all the harm and shame which it lies in my power to inflict upon you, as vassals who will not obey their lords. . . . And truly, whatsoever death and whatsoever misfortunes you in this wise may call down upon your heads, these will you owe to yourselves and neither to His Majesty, nor to me, nor to these knights who here surround me. And I hereby summon the notary to bear witness in writing to what I here have said to you and desired of you."

Thereupon the war began.

The Indians fought bravely and fiercely. But balls and powder are balls and powder, and Spanish steel is Spanish steel. Yet when the Indians had fled before the cannons and the guns, little gold remained in the houses of the abandoned town—a fact which brought the soldiers little joy. In return Cortez hewed three notches in the bark of a great tree in the midst of the town, and declared that the state of Tabasco was permanently occupied on behalf of the Catholic rulers of Spain—and that he would protect it against every assault and betrayal, with fire and the sword.

Thus began the train of victories against the treacherous redskins.

Already the next morning the Indians attempted their next act of treason against their new fatherland, Spain. But Cortez had already brought more horses, cannon, and men ashore from the ships; and by firing upon the traitors simultaneously from the front and from the rear he accomplished a bloodbath of imposing magnitude, destroying the cacao plantations and the fields of maize at the same time. Furthermore, the sight of the armored knights had a discouraging effect on the Aztecs' perfidious souls: since horses were unknown in the New World, they thought that beast and rider were one and the same being—with two heads, four eyes, and six iron-shod feet. The *Indios* were pursued with fire and steel to the Spaniards' battle cry: "*San Jago y San Pedro!*" The battle cry was so effective that both St. Peter and St.

James appeared in a cloud above the warriors, and helped to drive the heathens from Spain's new territory. At least one of the priests records this, but there must have been some dispute over the matter, for the old soldier Bernal Diaz related afterwards: "Great sinner that I am, on this occasion it was not given to me to gaze upon a single apostle."

Otherwise the bloodbath was thoroughly successful, and did not fail to have its effect on the surviving traitors and heathens. In addition Cortez—who in this year of Our Lord 1518 was himself thirty-five years old—now made the following proclamation of mercy: "I shall overlook and forgive what has passed, if you advise me forthwith of your total submission. Else I shall ride through the land and skewer every living being—man, woman, child—on my sword!"

"This was the first Christian proclamation of the Gospel to be made in New Spain," says the Dominican monk Las Casas, the same perfidious monk who later in such an un-Christian way took the part of the Indian heathens and traitors.

The next day a group of chieftains, followed by a train of slaves, came to Cortez to surrender to the general.

"The guilt for the bloodshed is on your own heads," declared Cortez thoughtfully; "but yet I shall deign to receive your gifts of gold and slaves—not least by reason of the twenty young slave girls who are to be found among the gifts." When the general and his men asked where all the gold came from, the chieftains pointed to the west and said: "Mexico."

The Christians were now burning with zeal to reach the interior of this land, where the fabled city of Mexico lay.

Cortez and his stalwarts were not the first Europeans to set their pious feet on Aztec soil. When Cuba, a few years earlier, had had a great shortage of slaves, a noble hidalgo by the name of Cordova had set forth on a slave-hunting journey around the islands. He was crossing from isle to isle, snapping up some children here, some women there, and some men both here and there, when he was interrupted in his pious errand by a raging storm which drove him to an unknown coast far to the west. When he went ashore he was met by natives clad in the very choicest and most fine-spun cotton, decorated with ornaments of braided gold. The natives lived, not in lean-tos or huts as on the islands, but in real stone houses several stories high. Unhappily they were cold and unfriendly to the strangers, and they spoke not one word of the Indian dialects common in Cuba and Hispaniola and on the islands. Finally these highly developed and civilized red-skins fell upon the Spaniards and drove them away, so that only just barely were the latter able to reach their ships and escape. With shivers of mortal dread mixed with Spanish thirst for gold, they afterwards told of this singular folk to the west. And they also had with them gold-adorned habits to prove that the story was true. This land of dreams was christened Yucatan.

And to Yucatan journeyed yet another proud youth, the hidalgo Grijalva, to harvest Indian souls for the Church's insatiable need of new converts to the true faith. Though he burned with holy fire for this great task, he had little success. He could confirm, however, that this was the land on which Columbus had been the very first to set foot, that it flowed with gold and riches, and that the natives did indeed build their houses in several stories and of stone. Among other things they found a white temple of stone, adorned with an altar full of severed human limbs from the last religious ceremony. The Spaniards were seized with terror at the sight, and hastened home to kneel before their own crucifixes bearing the twisted and tortured, bloody corpse of their own god, whom the Inquisition now served by torturing and thereafter maiming and burning men, women, and children alive. . . . The horror of the Aztecs' barbaric human sacrifices pursued them for a long time.

That same year the indomitable Cortez set out to convert the practitioners of human sacrifice, incorporate them into the Christian Church, and place the whole land under the protection of the Spanish King, as the monarch's rightful property. The converted *Indios* were then to confirm their submission to Spanish protection by sending His Christian Majesty the largest possible gifts of pearls, gold, and precious stones—and were thereafter to continue sending ever greater gifts to the Defender of the Faith in Seville.

When Cortez—the Great—went ashore in New Spain among the sacrificers of men, the process was set in motion; and from that day forward Spain's rulers could say with truth that the sun never set on their empire. It was the Cuban governor, Velasques, who outfitted Cortez with ships, arms, men, and horses; and from the time he weighed anchor in San Jago de Cuba, Cortez knew that, if Mexico lived up to its reputation, he would never divide the spoils and honor with his benefactor the governor, but would declare himself to be standing directly under His Majesty's protection, responsible solely to the King, and with no obligations whatsoever toward the governor who had made the expedition possible. Cortez was well prepared; he had been born, not on the islands, but home in the old Spain which had just expelled the Moorish armies, and which was now in the process of converting the Moslems and Jews of the realm to Christianity. The conversion was accomplished by dragging believing Arabs and Jews to the baptismal fonts where, against their will, they were baptized. But christened is christened; and if, after the baptism, the newly redeemed now persisted in their heathen beliefs, then they were no longer heathens, but *heretics*—which allowed the Christian Church to use the heresy laws and the courts and interrogation methods of the Inquisition against them. Jews and Arabs were duly tortured for weeks and months, and thereafter amid great festivity—and decked out in caps and bells—grilled alive to the delight of the populace and the clergy. In this way were burnt millions of converted infidels; and the transition from the Islamic hegemony to the Christian was great and pleasing to the Lord. Under the Arabs, Jews could be Jews and Christians Christians. Now there was an end to this atheistic laxity and indifference. The racks creaked, the thumbscrews squeaked, bones were crushed, and the pyres flamed. It was a time of greatness.

From this Spain came Hernando Cortez to Mexico.

It was not strange that he was disturbed by the Aztecs' human sacrifices and the priesthood's bloody rituals. *Into the baptismal font with them!* thought he, *it will make them better men*; and with the General, the distance between word and deed was never great. After the massacres of the defenseless Indians the survivors were duly baptized, for the soldiers had come to bring the Gospel to the redskins. The twenty virgins as well as the other slave girls were thoroughly enjoyed before the collective baptism took place, since unchastity with heathens is a far lesser sin than unchaste acts committed with baptized members of the community of the Lamb. That, at least, was how the shepherds saw it. All was happiness and joy among the crusaders. On Holy Thursday in the year of Our Lord 1519, Cortez's little fleet anchored off the island of Vera Cruz, still accompanied by the Cross. From the shore friendly natives came out to them in canoes and told them that they were in the land of the Aztecs, under the rule of the Aztecs' great emperor Montezuma, who lived in Mexico, the magnificent city of flowers behind the high mountains—and whose might and power were just as boundless as the Emperor's goodness. And Montezuma had heard of the white men's arrival, and bade his governor receive them with every royal courtesy and hospitality. Cortez replied that it was his will that none should suffer evil on account of the Spaniards' arrival, but that all should have great joy from it. Thereupon the heathen temples were torn down.

On Easter Sunday came the Aztec governor—haughty and proud, as representative of an empire he did not yet know was doomed.

"Where do you come from?" he said, "and why do you visit our shores?"

"From the king of kings," replied Cortez, "from the mightiest of all rulers on earth and in Heaven. It is His will that I visit Montezuma in person and bring him a message. When will I find him at home?"

"How can you think that you will be allowed to see the Emperor of the Aztecs?"

"I cannot leave this land without having spoken with Montezuma."

"I am surprised to hear that there exists a monarch who is as great and mighty as Montezuma. You shall receive a royal gift, and later you shall hear Montezuma's will."

The crusaders now received great gifts from the Emperor, borne by slaves—gold, fabrics of woven gold, precious stones and pearls, such that the pious men's eyes were like to fall out of their heads. In return they sent presents of copper and glass, along with a gilded chair, to Montezuma. The governor looked at a copper helmet and remarked that it resembled one of Montezuma's gold helmets—and Cortez gave it to him on the spot, with the proposal that he return it filled with gold dust—since he himself suffered from a heart diseases which could only be cured by gold. "If your ruler has gold, then bid him send me as much as possible."

The Aztec postal system was highly developed through a system of couriers who ran short relays and could thus maintain a high speed—and within twenty-four hours came an answer from Montezuma. There were new gifts of gold, precious stones, and works of art, and orders to leave the country at once. But Cortez had now founded the city of Vera Cruz, and nothing was farther from his mind than to leave a land which yielded such rich gifts, and which could offer Our Lord so many converted souls. He did not yet know how large the Aztecs' empire was, but he understood that it involved millions of subjects, all possessing gold and immortal souls.

At this point many had become impatient; for the first time Cortez hanged some of his own men. That improved the climate. But the troops were still restless, and thought that the division of spoils was being delayed a long time. Then Cortez, with some of his most loyal men, went down to the harbor and sank the ships, so that no one could think of returning home before Montezuma's riches belonged to them and the people had become Christian. Now there was no longer any choice: Mexico must be conquered.

The part of the story which follows is a story of powder and blood, of arms and cruelty. With the aid of steel and powder, Cortez's little criminal band of several hundred iron-clad Spaniards cut like a butcher knife through meat. They slew tens and hundreds of thousands. They bribed and bought cities and tribes which felt oppressed by the Aztec rule. Cortez became acquainted with Mexico's internal political situation; he gained allies, to whom he was faithful so long as it paid. The cities they came upon gradually got richer and richer and more and more beautiful, with gardens and houses and palaces of which the Europeans could never have dreamed. They saw irrigation systems in the form of great networks of canals through the cities, they saw zoological and botanical gardens, they saw buildings which towered against the clouds. And their fame preceded them; fear did its work. The Indians were paralyzed by the strangers' aspect. Of course, it was sometimes necessary to use force, and now and then the Aztecs put up such a fierce resistance that the Christians were just barely victorious. The gunpowder worked wonders.

And all the while they had to be on their guard against the faithless heathens, who would commit high treason and rebellion against His Majesty in Seville for a farthing—as if they hadn't understood that they themselves *belonged* to His Majesty, body and soul and possessions. The Spaniards were going easier on the conversions now. They had gained many, many allies, whom they would lose if they tried to convert them into the bargain. Christ could wait. He was used to it.

In return they reaped gold, jewels, and valuables beyond their wildest dreams; but that didn't concern Christ, who had never bothered about that sort of thing, and had preferred to live in poverty among men. So at least they weren't cheating Him out of anything, since He didn't want it anyway. The Church, on the other hand, would accept it.

But the expedition to the mysterious hinterland was no Sunday outing, powder and steel notwithstanding. The Indians' will to fight, their courage, and their enormous number made it difficult to be a Christian in those days. The worst was the republic of Tlascala, which, despite the fact that it was an enemy of Montezuma and the Aztecs, still put up the fiercest resistance against the Spaniards. Time after time they barely escaped with their lives. And they remembered these encounters for centuries afterwards. But they went on and on. They came from Spain, and they had learned to deal with heathens. When they stood outside the city, the capital of the republic of Tlascala, they thought at first that what they saw wasn't a city, but a piece of Heaven in all its beauty. There were imposing towers of white stone; there were gardens, palaces, dwellings, and temples without equal—not even the Moors had built cities like these. Add to this a population so freedom-loving, and so skilled in battle, that even Montezuma's armies had been unable to subdue them. But the Spaniards had an ally they didn't know about. In the Aztec kingdom there was an ancient prophecy that there would one day come white gods over the sea from an empire to the east; and when these warrior-gods came, Aztec Mexico's days would be numbered. The gods would bring its destruction. This the Spaniards knew nothing about, but for a long time the legend worked like a poison in the Aztecs' blood; it paralyzed them, right up until they saw that the whites weren't gods, but merely thugs—and that they had no other religion than gold.

The city of Tlascala lay like a jewel before Cortez and his men, gleaming with unimaginable riches. And the terror of the whites had preceded them; after continual new defeats the *Indios* began to believe that the strangers were truly invincible—and the republicans decided to become the whites' allies against Montezuma. Therefore they sent out forty venerable envoys to make the Christians a declaration of their friendship and their readiness to join them in the fight against the Aztecs and Montezuma's enormous realm.

But Cortez wasn't one to put unnecessary trust in the word of heathens and treacherous Indians. An intimate scene took place. The forty venerable men were bound, and put up no resistance—since they were unarmed, and had come in friendship and peace. Cortez caused a large block of wood to be erected, and beside it a big kettle of oil was put over the fire. Then the work began. And they needed many men to finish it in the course of a day. And each of the forty defenseless worthies had *two* hands. For awhile Cortez brooded over whether it would suffice to take just one hand from each, but he concluded that two are better than one.

Only in the afternoon was the work finished. And on the earth around the block lay eighty severed hands. It had taken some time, for it was simultaneously a surgical task: the stumps of the arms had to be dipped one by one into the boiling oil to close the veins, and the blood must be stanched thoroughly. On top of this many of the perfidious redskins didn't like the procedure and put up a resistance, during both the amputation and the oil bath afterwards. They were disobedient.

But before darkness fell all forty could be chased back to Tlascala as examples of how traitors would be treated. They were able to return home on foot.

As was to be expected, the incident made a certain impression on them. The eighty hands were thrown together in a big heap and buried on the spot. Now everyone knew who had the power in Tlascala.

The next day the reconciliation was completed; all were now friends, and the Spaniards marched into the city. The Tlascalans proved to be tough opponents and faithful friends. From now on they stuck with Cortez through thick and thin.

Now there came a new greeting from Montezuma, who had heard of the victory over the invincible republic of Tlascala. He sent his heartiest greetings, along with enormous treasures—gold and jewels in almost limitless quantities, with a promise of much, much more if the Spaniards would leave the country again by the same way they had come. But Cortez didn't want *much*; he wanted *all*. "It is impossible for

me to leave this blessed land without having personally paid
homage to the great Montezuma. I must see the emperor's
face in all its splendor."

Their sojourn in the city of Tlascala was pleasant. By the
time they marched in, every trace of hostility had disappeared. The eighty hands had done their work. The city was
even more overwhelming when seen from inside than from a
distance. On the housetops lay gardens with the most exquis-
ite combinations of flowers and plants; in doors and windows
hung the most marvelous draperies of cloth of gold, with silver bells to warn of visitors. In the streets and at the market-
places there were shops by the hundreds, and scattered
around the city the most luxurious public baths. The police
functioned discreetly but effectively to maintain law and
order in the city, and the hairdressing salons and beauty par-
lors were of unsurpassed quality. Many Spaniards married
young Indian women, who often brought enormous dowries
in addition to their beauty and amiability. The brave, golden-
haired, and fair-skinned Alvadaro married a daughter of one
of the chieftains and won the Indians' affection, along with
the name "Tonatiuh," which means "the sun." He would one
day be just as hated as he was now beloved.

Now came the awaited message from the Emperor.
Montezuma again sent gold and gifts, but he begged them not
to abide in the barbaric and underdeveloped Tlascala, but to
come to Mexico—after first betaking themselves to the relatively civilized city of Cholula, whence they would be fetched
by a noble escort. The Tlascalans protested and said that all
Aztecs had false hearts—or none at all—and begged their
white friends to remain with them until the attack on Montezuma's capital itself could be mounted. But Cortez knew what
he wanted, and took with him six thousand Tlascalan warriors to the city of Cholula.

Cholula was a city which made Tlascala look like a poor
farm. The wealth was enormous, but employed with taste and
a matchless sense of beauty. However, Cholula refused to
allow the Tlascalans within its walls, despite the fact that the

whites were received with hospitality. This awakened Cortez's suspicions, and he decided to set an example which should forever after make every *Indio* blanch at the very word "Spaniard." Cavalier that he was, Cortez now invited all the city's chieftains and nobles to visit him in the castle yard where he and his men were guests. It was a palace without equal, filled not only with precious stones and gold and costly treasures, but also with the most wondrous flowers, animals, birds, snakes, monsters—things which no Christian eye had ever before beheld. In this palace Cortez had installed himself with several hundred steel-clad men. And thither, to the palace yard, came all the leaders of the city of Cholula. They were clad in festive clothes, in noble raiment, in jewels and in everything the human heart desires, in gold and silver and precious stones without end—but naturally, because of their friendship with the Christians, unarmed. Cortez was still intoxicated from his meeting with the city's riches and splendors, and had just written to his monarch that "no city in Spain can compare with Cholula in beauty, with all its towers and with the enormous luxury enjoyed by all of the inhabitants. . . ."

The city's unarmed dignitaries gathered by the thousands in the courtyard, and then the gates were closed behind them. The Christians had muskets, pistols, cannons, armor, and above all their good Spanish swords, of the hardest steel and razor-sharp. The city's treachery could not be left unpunished, declared Cortez, and therewith came the crack of the first shot. None escaped. The confined guests were one big lump of flesh, and the cannons, loaded with spikes, pieces of iron, scrap iron, and stones, fired again and again into the crowd. The Spaniards went bravely to the attack with musket and pistol and sword, and they say that the blood flowed like rainwater after a day in the wet season. The panic and rage in the city outside the walls was boundless, but of no avail. Those who survived the massacre were collected afterwards and made to wait until the Spaniards had gotten together enough wood. Then they were bound and laid on the pyres and burned alive. This was a method of execution to which the Europeans always returned when they were forced to punish traitors of this sort. It was of great interest to ascertain that the false gods of the *Indios* did not interfere to save them as they lay screaming on the pyres.

Cortez now traveled on towards Mexico City.

And nothing stopped him. Again it was a difficult journey, over high mountains and narrow passes, through rain and wind and at times through snowstorms—for, despite their southerly situation, the mountains are so high that snowstorms are to be met with in summer as well as winter. Crossing them was hard for the Spaniards, and it was fatal to many of their Indian allies. But they got through, and one day Mexico lay between the five lakes at their feet, down in a valley so unimaginably lovely and rich that many of the Spaniards thought that this must be Paradise; it could no longer be an earthly land.

Woods, gardens, fields and plantations, canals for irrigation and for transport; in the lakes, the beautiful floating islands which the Aztecs so loved; and in the midst of all this, Mexico—city of white towers and temples, gardens, palaces, and all that may delight the human eye.

Once again the city contained things which no European had ever beheld before—botanical and zoological gardens, but bigger, richer, and more splendid than those achieved by any other Mexican city. Special mention is made of the birdhouse, containing thousands of songbirds and birds of prey. The Moors' Alhambra, their Medinas and their mosques, as well as the Christian cathedrals and castles—all paled beside what the Spaniards here beheld.

Two years later, not a stone remained. The fields were dried out, the plantations scorched by the sun, the canals empty, the dikes ruined, the cities leveled to the ground, the gardens trampled down, the palaces smashed, the temples burned, the animals slain, the Emperor dead, the people murdered, children and women ravished and killed. All was death and disaster. The whites had come.

It happened thus:

The Spaniards stood as if dumbstruck, gazing down into the valley; and they saw what no European eye had beheld—a glory which made them think that they were not witnessing earthly splendors, but standing before Paradise itself. Not even in China or in India had white men seen the like. The Christians now understood that before them they were seeing the reward of all their toil, of sweat and frost, of hunger and thirst—an earthly paradise toward which they had now been struggling for months, cutting and shooting their way through primeval forests and human flesh. Beneath them five lakes lay glittering in the sunshine, and along all the beaches were gleaming cities with white spires and flowers, flowers, flowers. Behind the biggest of the lakes lay Chapoltepec, its hills and ridges covered with cypresses and gardens; but in the midst of everything, among the white towers, the temples, the lakes, the floating islands—in a sun of glittering water—lay the dream city, the capital city of temples and palaces, surrounded by the five lakes in a veil of sunshine and purple: the city Tenochtitlan, the city Mexico, the capital of the Promised Land.

The Christians looked down into the valleys and across the golden cornfields, the green forests, and the glittering canals—and they were filled with a great joy: the consciousness that the glory of Christ had been vested in St. Peter and the Holy See, and thence passed on to His most Catholic Majesty and ruler over Spain—and from the ruler, on to those who served the ruler's will. It was staggering to know that everything they saw at their feet now rightfully belonged to them—that all this magnificence, splendor, and wealth was their own property, of which they were now to take legal possession. The rejoicing among the soldiers was great; and among the officers, to whom were allotted higher quotas of heathen and barbarian property, the joy was—if possible— even greater. They all looked down into the valley toward the lakes, the cities, the towers, the palaces, the gardens, and the temples—and all were thinking: what gold, gems, and treasures are not to be found *within* these towers, temples, places, and dwellings? And they understood that the Lord's blessing was with them.

Then they journeyed down into the valley, plundering, laying waste, ravishing, and amusing themselves. And now the miracle happened. Mexico—under the leadership of Montezuma, the great emperor—put up no defense. So terrible was the fame which had preceded the intruders that the Aztecs, the ruling nation, bowed their heads at the sight of the first white men. And a European host of several hundred men with firearms marched straight into the capital city with its many hundreds of thousands, perhaps millions, of inhabitants, without anyone's lifting a finger in his own defense.

Everything could have happened otherwise; the Aztecs could have crushed the intruders the very day they showed their faces. Now they received them as friends. The whites brought their horses and cannons with them into the city, and they occupied Mexico's ancient palace, which they quickly rebuilt into a fortress.

Amid gifts and proofs of friendship from the emperor they made themselves at home. But Cortez would not have been Cortez had he not seen the Spaniards' hopeless position: surrounded by an enemy which could crush them at any time by virtue of these millions of inhabitants, the Spaniards were at the Aztecs' mercy, even with their firearms and their Spanish steel. All around them, hundreds of thousands of red warriors stood ready to take up spear and sword the moment the Emperor Montezuma commanded it.

But Montezuma gave no command; he received his European gods with the greatest cordiality and treated them as brothers. The little group of Europeans penetrated to the land's very heart, they lived in the Emperor's palace, they held untrammeled sway over the land. They decided everything. And when the moment was come, they took the Emperor prisoner and held him hostage. No gangsters, no Al Capone, no Dillinger could have done a better job. By threatening to execute the holy Emperor, the god and ruler, they forced the Aztecs' total compliance with the white men's will. The Spaniards had captured the palace; they had the Emperor's life in their hands; and they decided, so to speak, what should be on the palace menu. The Emperor bowed his head and bore the Europeans' conduct not only humbly, but also with the greatest cheerfulness. All were attentive to the Spaniards' slightest wishes. And they knew that the life of their Emperor and their god lay in the white men's bloody hands. Never had the Aztec empire been subjected to a greater humiliation and abasement.

In truth the Spaniards' situation was desperate; should Montezuma die a natural death, they would no longer have a hostage. Therefore they took his brother and his nephew and a number of his relatives prisoner. And when the treacherous *indios* at the coast rebelled and committed high treason, they took the opportunity to make examples of the guilty: Aztec nobles and their next of kin, seventeen in all, were ceremoniously convicted of rebellion against His Catholic Majesty, and in one of Mexico's great public squares wood and logs were gathered for a great and highly Christian bonfire. The white gods from the East now showed their power.

The seventeen Aztecs mounted the pyre with the greatest serenity, and allowed themselves to be burned alive.

Now, too, the Emperor's coffers were discovered; and to show his good will, Montezuma allowed all his gold and everything he received from his subjects to be sent to the Catholic Majesty in Seville. There were shiploads of gold and gems, riches which were of great benefit to the Majesty's European bank accounts.

Now the looting of Mexico began.

All might have been well had not Cortez been forced to go off to suppress a rebellion among the Spanish soldiers at the coast. They hadn't gotten enough gold, and wanted to return home to Cuba. As his deputy in Mexico he left the faithful Alvadaro, he who, by reason of his golden hair and beard and his fair skin, was called by the Indians "Tonatiuh"—The Sun.

While The Sun ruled Mexico alone and by the grace of God, he chanced to remember the massacre in Cholula, and he remembered it fondly. When he heard rumors of discontent and treachery among the inhabitants, he summoned all the city's great and prominent men to a meeting in the courtyard inside the palace. They came as to a feast, and even the divine Montezuma was present—of course without knowing of Tonatiuh's plans. The gates were locked, the sedition act read aloud in Spanish, the cannons wheeled into position, the bloodbath begun: it is related that in their despair a number of the Aztecs tried to scale the vertical stone walls, but Spanish guards were standing on top and chopped off their hands, so that they fell back into the mess of blood inside the courtyard. Hundreds and hundreds were killed, but even as the last screams sounded from the mangled inside the palace courtyard, the people began gathering outside. That highly special red juice which flowed proved literally to be the bloody drops which made the cup run over.

Mexico rose up in rebellion, and the whites were confined to the area of the palace. The Emperor's life was their sole pawn and hostage. Cortez returned and declared that Alvadaro—The Sun—was an idiot, and that almost all of their careful, heroic groundwork was labor wasted and thrown away. He had to pull the chestnuts out of the fire which Alvadaro had lit.

With the pitiful remnants of his band of murderers, Cortez, the military genius, crawled out of Mexico. The departure took place at night, after Mexico's inhabitants had stoned their emperor Montezuma as he stood on the castle battlements and begged them to let the white gods reign in peace. Now all was darkness, blood, and flame.

It was one of the greatest nights in the history of the human race. But the whites escaped from the city.

Montezuma's last words were these: "You have destroyed my empire and my people whom I love above all else on earth. But I bear you no malice."

Once the Emperor was dead, all that mattered to the

Spaniards was to get out of the city between the five lakes. And they managed.

Before a year had passed they returned to punish the traitors—and here begins the history of Mexico's obliteration. Systematically, step by step, the Christians subdued every city along the shores of the five lakes. The memory of that last terrible night never left them—and among the Spaniards it is still called "la noche triste" to this very day. They knew that they had returned to take vengeance, and it was accomplished.

Once the lakes and the shores were under control, it was the turn of Mexico City itself. It was now surrounded and besieged.

Here it is necessary to go back to the very first black man who brought chicken pox ashore on the North American continent. The disease made itself useful. It spread like fire in dry grass, and brought with it plague and famine. But the red men fought like devils. Time after time the Spaniards were driven back over dikes and bridges and lakes. Yet they came closer and closer, inch by inch. The whites filled the canals and straits with torn-down houses and towers and palaces. Very slowly, day by day, Mexico was leveled to the ground in the most literal sense. The city became *flat*.

After Montezuma's death the Aztecs had chosen his brother Guatemozin—a man who had never trusted the white men's word and promises—as emperor. He was leading them now. And the lakes were filled with the dead.

No one has succeeded in describing the battle. Suffice it to say that toward the end, one could walk through the whole city on dead Indians. There were districts where one couldn't set foot on the ground. Men, women, and children covered the whole area around the palace in several layers. The natives died of plague, disease, and hunger; and block by block the city was burned and plundered—houses burned with the sick and wounded inside. The last massacre surpassed anything the Spaniards had known; finally even the priests felt pity for the heathens. Now the stink of corpses filled the whole valley around the five lakes, and all the fields and plantations were destroyed. The canals were without water, and the cornfields and the gardens lay dead, scorched black by the sun.

The emperor was taken alive; he was promised safe-conduct and royal treatment during his imprisonment. Thereupon he and the other survivors were subjected to torture, a science the Christians knew something about. But the Spaniards had already appropriated all the gold they could possibly lay their hands on, all the precious stones and all the riches which were to be found. Finally, for the sake of order, the emperor was hanged. The allied Indian tribes who had fought with the whites against the Aztecs were now enslaved, and under Spanish whips they tried to rebuild the city. The work was hard, and many of the enslaved died of hunger and overwork. Even the Spanish enlisted men were cheated out of the gold they had expected, and received the Indians' land instead—which didn't much please them, even if they could work it with the former owners as slaves. Cortez was named royal governor, supreme judge, and sole ruler over the whole kingdom of Mexico. With the law in his hand, he now affirmed that all Indians were and should remain true slaves—whereupon they were baptized. The population forthwith put all its strength into dying out—an art form splendidly developed among higher cultures which are conquered by lower ones. Afterwards, by order of the clergy, all Aztec writings—and with them Mexico's historical records—were burned. Not only were the land and the city destroyed, but temples, buildings, and all visible culture were as far as possible wiped off the face of the earth. About the same time the kingdom of Peru suffered the fate of being discovered by Pizarro, after it had lain there for thousands of years without anyone's setting eyes upon it. The Incas had been discovered only by themselves. They were now attacked, lied to, deceived, and finally subdued by the Christians. The land was richer than Mexico, and the Incas had just as high a culture as the Aztecs. They suffered the same fate after their meeting with firearms and Christianity: the land was laid waste and plundered of all its gold and riches. Peru too was made as uninhabitable as possible. It was then Christianized.

Cortez died at the age of sixty-two in Spain, after his Lord and King had relieved him of his position as governor in the far West. His last words were that he wanted to go home to Mexico— "to settle his account with God. . . ."

"It is far," he said.

Then he died a Christian syphilitic's death in God's name. His work was done: Paradise was a desert. In thirty years nineteen million had been slaughtered. It isn't given to everyone to destroy a culture.

I walk alone a great deal here. These lonely wanderings through the city are my great joy. Perhaps that's my only joy, to be alone. I could go out into the desert and howl like a dog, but the jackals are also good at howling, and the desert is no longer what it was. There are so many who have cried in the wilderness without its bringing any change in earthly conditions. When I'm on these walks, my childhood comes uncannily near. And it's the only thing which is mine alone. My own interior is the only thing which belongs solely to me. It's impossible to write such a precise record that I can share it with others.

What is it that makes me so totally incapable of adjusting to this world? Not even as a child could I manage—even though I've been told that I was an unusually good and tractable creature, until I'd been going to school for a couple of years. I must have changed suddenly in the course of a few days. After that I was incorrigible. It's only this period of active resistance which I can really remember. I could drive a teacher into a rage, get myself thrown out of class, just by staring at him with a determined look. I regarded it as a given that the whole world outside me was unbearably hostile—it wanted to do something to me which I absolutely didn't want. The police, the military, the church, the whole society was hostile—and school was their exponent. School was the front line where I met the enemy face to face. Here I had them all within range, here the strength of the individual versus the rest of the world could be tested. Here we fought the preliminary skirmishes over how this world was, the world they were defending and saw fit to keep as little changed as possible, as much as possible the way it was—with king, queen, madhouse, Wrigley's chewing gum, the holy catholic Church and the whole pigsty. Already from the time I was around ten years old, that's what the world looked like to me: a sty pure and simple. In this pigpen it was always the coarsest, the greediest, the most brazen, the most hypocritical who had the power, and the power was exercised through the most stupid and brutal: through teachers, priests, policemen, judges, and sergeants. And in this sty I would have to go on living—for perhaps another seventy years?

My school days I perceived intuitively as one long humiliation. The only time classes were fun was when we were shown slides, and half the class would sit in pairs and jerk each other off in the dark.

One of my last years in grade school—in sixth or seventh grade—I experienced a scene which, though utterly insignificant, still made a powerful impact on me. We had a really kind and good teacher, I think I can say a truly good and benevolent example of the species; he was our homeroom teacher, and on this day he was giving us religious instruction. For some reason he was speaking on the theme that it is God who thinks for us and in us—and through us. (Of course the thought is profound if one means something deeper by "God," but there was no question of that here; it was Luther's old, feebleminded, brutal God he was talking about.) He was wrought up and in dead earnest as he presented this idiotic twaddle to a flock of children, and I immediately felt the insanity in it: at that moment God was thinking quite differently in me than in him, and it was almost embarrassing to picture poor old God having such thoughts as I went around with. If my good, kind teacher could have known for only a minute what kind of thoughts most often entered my head, he would have reacted differently to what happened now. Very loudly, and in fact with a kind of dismay, I said:

"Does he think for me too?"

Our kind old teacher parted his lips as if he were going to smile, and I saw his long yellow teeth surrounded by foam at the corners of his mouth. But he didn't smile, he bared his teeth like an animal about to bite. Then he shrieked, spraying spit out over the class:

"Yes, God thinks for you too!"

I'd never dreamed that that proper and pious man could be so carried away with rage. He used the pointer not only to strike with, but also to stab with—in other words as a sharp instrument, which was much more refined. Then I was standing out in the hall where I belonged, and where I felt much better. I was aware that I had touched something in the man's innermost being—but what was *that?* What *was* his innermost being? It was hardly the rabbi Joshua who dwelt in his pious old teacher's heart. What the devil really dwells inside such a man?

What dwells inside any of us?

It isn't just lilies and roses which grow in the Mary's gardens of our hearts. Two or three years after the pointer episode I began my first protocol, in the drama's deathless, highly concentrated form. Unfortunately the manuscript is lost to posterity, and only fragments remain in my rather worn and perforated memory. The drama was set in the Kingdom of Heaven, and took the form of a family drama within the framework of the Holy Trinity. Even in my play God's Son was viewed within the context of established theology; he was conceived through a proxy of the Holy Ghost— and His Father, in other words the principal of both, was arrayed in a beard and a floor-length gown. He was immeasurably old, and a complete imbecile. God was in his second childhood in my first play. Today it would have been called a searching minidrama for three characters, easy to produce in the bourgeois stage's advanced little theaters. The original thing in the conception was that between Jesus and the Holy Ghost there existed a highly obscene sexual incongruity, in that the former was incessantly being abused by the Holy Ghost—abused per anum, but without being able to achieve reciprocal anal contact. In spite of this, large parts of the Holy Ghost's anal activities took place on the open stage.

One day God comes in and catches them in the act. From this arose many complications and difficulties in the plot—which, however, were all resolved in one stroke, with all the characters—*tous les trois ensembles*—mutually satisfying their needs at once, in approximately the same fashion as a class of boys during a slide show. But on stage and with the lights on.

How can it be that it's God "who thinks for me" when such a young author forms that kind of thoughts about the hereafter and eternal life? I remember that I copied the drama out neatly in a manuscript of something over twenty pages. Several of my friends had a great time reading it, but as I said, it was never performed. Now the papers are lost, along with all the thousands of other things drowned in the river of time.

Shortly after the composition of the abovementioned play I was officially expelled from school for the first time. I was a first-year student in a high school which is still adorned with the name of its founder—my great-great-grandfather, who was a bishop in that part of the country where I was later born. There's a bad omen in this: my first expulsion was not due to my actions or manifestations of criminality; it was because of untoward freedom of expression in my written work that I was shown the door of the school founded by my blessed great-great-grandfather. I was seventeen the first time I was cast out of society for having given my candid opinion written form. Since then I can only regret that my teachers weren't also presented with the drama about the Holy Trinity. When still at a young age I should have been burned on top of my protocols. But at that time it was no longer the fashion, even if it was in the thirties.

Our class was obliged, during the Pentecost vacation, to spend a whole Friday sitting indoors on a sunny day and writing a theme as a punishment. Our assignment was to write about Alexander the Great, but I no longer remember what joint crime had occasioned the collective expiation. As ungodly and dangerous seventeen-year-olds we had certainly—seen against the background of contemporary history, Hitler's orgies in Germany and Stalin's trials in Moscow—been guilty of dreadful things. I just don't know what. But the point is that while the blood was flowing from the honorable courts in Germania and Russia, we must have sinned; at any rate, we were sitting there doing time together. So I don't remember the crime, but I do remember the theme we had to write.

By pure coincidence, and because by then I had already had become addicted to the reading of books to a shameful degree, I had studied Alexander's history on my own—in Plutarch among other writers. In short, I wrote that Alexander was a faggot and a murderer and had been converted to the Egyptian mysteries through "experience with/of God" (I remember the wording exactly, even after thirty-five years). To this were added certain insights into Alexander's sexual practices and extravagances. A teacher from the school's stable had been assigned to monitor the class—and he belonged to a strange religious sect which, under the name of "the Oxford Movement," was plaguing Europe at the time. The religious sports terminology of this movement likewise included the expression "experience *with or of* God." The teacher was green, dumb, and newly converted. In my innocence I asked permission, when the composition was finished, to go outside and relieve myself before revising it. The minute I left the classroom, that fat, godly little eunuch of a university-educated idiot went and sat down at my desk, where he read through my theme with the zeal of an apostle. He returned gravely to his cathedra and placed his hemorrhoids on the worn, shiny seat of the chair. Great things had come to pass, and the Lord had inspired him with mighty thoughts. He knew that a momentous hour was come; he was to strike a blow for God! Ah, how would God have managed without the aid of our teacher? In his finest script, with his small soft hands which had never held a hammer or an axe, he wrote his report in the class record.

Three days later I was a free and happy young man; for the first time in my whole childhood expelled from school, liberated from daily attendance at the pigsty.

I was forcibly enrolled in other schools, but now I had learned the art of being expelled, and I made use of it. In town after town I was cast out of the ranks of future academic citizens.

At this point stands one of the catastrophes of my life. Not an external one, but an internal one, a defeat which still torments me more than almost anything else. With a friend I planned to get myself over to England and stay there, but at the last minute I lost my nerve. I've thought about this for decades since—about how my not daring to cut and run from it all was to stamp my whole life. In fact, I think that a choice at the age of seventeen showed that something in me was wrong, that the stuff I was made of was too weak and soft—that something had begun to rot already back then. I was quite simply afraid.

Had I done it, everything would have been different through all the decades which were to come.

That I chickened out of running away stands for me to this very day as my greatest moral defeat. My friend did get over to England two or three years later, and eventually fell in the war.

In this choice I met for the first time the things which I hate and despise in myself: compliancy, indolence, duplicity, all the things which should have been burned out with a hydrogen flame before they succeeded in poisoning all that I was or could have become. I walk around the streets of this African city thinking about this, and as a trained executioner I do it thoroughly.

It's strange, and it happens again and again: I'm walking along thinking over my life, and when I come to this point, I eventually discover that I'm not *walking* anymore. I've stopped dead, in the midst of the traffic, in the middle of the sidewalk; people are walking all around me, and I'm standing motionless, looking down at the asphalt, right in front of my feet. I just stand there, not thinking; but *seeing.* I see before me again that damned accursed little boy, with the long black curls, the oversized head, the round belly, and the thin legs. I don't *think* of him. I *see* him. I smell him. He's present in everything. When I was too cowardly to leave the country, and in a thousand other situations, it was that nice, scared little boy, that tractable, friendly, and polite boy who had gotten the upper hand.

The boy from before the third grade in primary school.

He who acted as if he had adjusted, acted as if he felt at home in the sty and liked to wallow in the excreta of the bourgeoisie. He pretended he'd never known the boy who said what he thought, who did what he wanted, who would be downright disobedient rather than change his opinion—who got himself expelled from school after school. This nice little boy is the only real enemy I have.

I discover that I'm standing still in the middle of the sidewalk, right in front of all the busy people with their justified existences who are on the way *from* something *to* something. I'm standing in front of the stone balustrade on the great promenade which in curve after curve leads down to the center, to the actual city. There's nobody else here who goes the whole way on foot. Even the beggars will sit at the bus stops and beg to be taken along gratis, and the Moslems have their duties to Allah; they often buy tickets for the poor. So I walk this long, stone-paved road alone, past palms and cedars and stone pines, utterly and entirely alone, just as I've always done. How did I get this way?

Was it the meeting with the world, which I may have perceived with bloodier nerves than most people? Is it sickness, or is it health?

I have decided that it is health.

It is *I* who am well, the others are sick.

Why, twenty years ago, did I begin to write this protocol about *bestialitetens historie,* about *de Geschichte de la cruauté,* about *l'histoire der Grausamkeit,* the history of *bestialité,* *la storia*

of cruelty? It will never be written, because it has no beginning and no end. How on earth can one imagine a continua-
tion of world history without cruelty, how could one envision
the rise of a society without cruelty as its innermost, sustain-
ing principle—as society's basic idea?

It's here that the sickness lies. *We just can't imagine a world
without bestiality as the rulers' final argument!* We can't imagine
a society which doesn't build on brute force.

I've talked quite a bit with God about this, and even if he's
often evasive, it's still possible to get him into a corner if one
is just ruthless enough.

Once I met him, strangely enough, by the Cestius pyra-
mid in Rome, and he was very low, almost heartbroken. So I
took him into the Protestant churchyard and sat him on a
bench under the rustle of the mighty treetops. It's odd to be
in this space with all those Protestant, blond Nordic names, in
the middle of a great Catholic city—and it was especially
strange to be sitting there with God. Here lie many of the
Great Dead, and many who aren't so great, but who are
nonetheless dead.

"What do you think about Protestants and Catholics,
God?"

He looked up, with eyes of darkest brown under his
ancient forehead and white eyebrows. He was dressed simply, almost shabbily, and you could have taken him for an
old street vendor, but he didn't have any pushcart. I was the
only one who recognized him.

"I don't think anything about them," he replied; "it's they
who think something about me."

I observed him sharply to see if he was smiling, but there
was no sign of it. He sat motionless looking straight ahead, in
between the trees and the graves. Then he said:

"But I know what *you* think about them, and that's
enough."

The treetops sighed with a wind from the sea, all the way
from Ostia. Suddenly it smelled of ocean and clams and mussels. All the glory of a newly-created world lay fresh and

unspoiled in this breath of wind. God sniffed the sea air.

"Shall we go and have some lunch?" I asked. "I know a little *trattoria* nearby which always has fresh seafood at this time."

"I don't have any money," said God.

I told him that I had money for us both, and we got to our feet (neither of us is especially nimble-footed anymore), tottered across a couple of small streets, and found ourselves a place inside the cool shady room among the white, newly-ironed tablecloths. It was just before the stream of native luncheon guests usually arrived, and all the places were set with bread and plates. I ordered *frutta di mare* to begin with, and a light, dry wine from the mountains.

"Why are you so nice to me?" asked God.

"Strictly speaking, it's you who have created both shrimp and scampi and crayfish, and let's not forget the tiny squid, fried to a crisp—I especially want to mention them. Furthermore, you've also created the white wine and the casks it's tapped from . . . so it's really yours, all if it."

"There aren't many who think like that anymore," answered God. He nodded in the same way as Columbus— slowly and thoughtfully, with the same expression in his eyes as the great admiral has. Both of them do that when they're seeing pictures inside themselves, pictures which only they know about. After the hors d'œuvres we ordered more wine, fish fillets, and a salad of white beans.

"Oh, God!" I sighed.

"Yes?" he said.

"It's just that it tastes so damned good," I replied. "It doesn't often happen anymore that food tastes good to me. My appetite disappears after a mouthful or two; the food is no longer what it was. Weeks can go by in which I can hardly get down anything but bread and cheese. But today the food was tasty. That's why I took your name in vain—out of contentment."

"It concerns me that you're losing your appetite. Do you have pain in your belly?"

"Yes," I replied, "I always have pain in my belly. Every day."

"What do the doctors say about it?"

"Not much. Just that I have a chronic intestinal catarrh—and so do a lot of people. It's something one is born with if one doesn't feel at home on this earth. The doctors say that I must have had it since I was a small child, and it's true. But when I was in my prime I could eat all I wanted anyway."

"It's not because you've abused my gifts?"

He nodded gravely at the fish, lemons, oil, and wine.

"Only partly."

He sat for a while in thought. Then he said:

"Can't you have done with *The History of Bestiality?* That's what's ruining your appetite and your digestion. If you're going to sit thinking of newly-scalded children every time you eat a crayfish tail, no good can come if it. Have done with the misery!"

"I'll never stop!" I said. "You won't get off so easily!"

Now he was no longer just an ordinary doddering gaffer who looked like a street vendor. He was wide awake—a strong, robust, and athletic old man. He was on the defensive.

"Stop what you're working on," he replied; "then you'll get back both your appetite and your good digestion. The earth shall be yours! I'll make you rich and get you a job with a broadcasting company or a rich publisher. I'll give you health, wealth, and a salaried position with UNESCO. It's good for a man of letters to be a bit critical, but there must be limits to everything. Somewhere you must *fall on your knees and worship!* It doesn't matter whom you kneel to, whom you worship—you can face east or west, north or south. *But fall on your knees and worship—and this world shall be yours!*"

"You aren't God," I said. "You have a tail."

"Only *one* is almighty. I lay the world at your feet."

"I shit on the world. Get thee behind me, Satan."

Then I was sitting alone again, eating a dessert of nuts and figs.

Since then I've met him again, though he avoids me. This decisive meeting in Rome took place several years ago, and my digestion hasn't improved since then. I can eat properly only when I'm perfectly relaxed and totally alone, and have lots of wine to wash the food down with. It looks as if all earthly joys go their way.

Now—as we write in the year 519 after Columbus—I've met God again here in the desert, and he spoke to me from a fig tree and said:

"*Worship, and you yourself shall be worshiped!*"

It's strange how old this thought is: You must own the world, you must be worshiped. But first you yourself must kneel and worship one of this world's princes. Even God or the Great Prince can't imagine your having other interests than gold and adoration, wealth and fame. I've told God that he'll have to come up with other temptations than these—but the only alternative is that he says he can make my stomach well again, if I'll kneel down and worship. Of course that means a lot, but not enough. And when it comes to gold and glory, I must admit that I understand the temptation; but I don't want more than enough to pay my bills and keep food and drink in the house.

Actually, it's striking what small sums people can be bought for. Even in cases where not a speck of idealism enters the picture, the history of espionage shows that hardly any amount is too small, and no great power needs to dig very deeply into its billions to pay its agents in other countries. One of the most instructive spy stories I know comes from dear old Switzerland, from the free republic formed in the meadow at Rütli. This spy story is little and gray and sad, and no middle-class magazine or publisher would think of bringing it out as a book or a serial. It's much too true, much too small, and much too gray. It doesn't involve any spy who came in from the cold or the dark or whatever. It merely involves a quiet and timorous little Swiss, a weary and faithful husband and father, who became more and more afraid of his wife. He belonged to the many who had gotten a relatively good start in life. To begin with. After passing his law exam with an average grade, he got an entry-level job in the Defense Department, and all went

well. But the promotions failed to come. He received little gold
and even less glory. In short, he was miserable, and as the
years went by he looked more and more wretched—in worn
but clean clothes, with narrow shoulders, and progressively
battered by life, ever more bowed and bent. No aura of excite-
ment and exotic lands surrounded him. To talk of freedom,
eagle eyes, and adventure in connection with this spy makes
little sense. He had less of the carnivore in him than most people; but still he had his small, meager but secure salary. When
he brought it home it was confiscated by his wife, who knew
what was best for everybody. He was given his weekly
allowance of fourteen francs, and the rest went into the increas-
ingly Spartan housekeeping, except for a certain sum which
was put in the bank for their children's education and dowry.
Thus the years went by, and every day he walked between
home and office, just as terrified of his wife as of his boss.

But what nobody knew, no one suspected—was that he
had a secret, he carried with him a dream, a dream which
could become great and volatile as the wind, strong and
warm as the foehn storms in his home village up in the
Alpine valleys. It gripped him around the chest and bore him
up, far, far, away—away from the everyday, away from the
dread of wife and boss, far, far into a golden land of sunshine
and flowers and sea and vaulted sky. In short: *he drank.*

God knows he was no titanic drinker, storming the gates
of heaven; he wasn't one to wave his broad-brimmed hat and
sail off on the shifting winds of evening. He was a truly gentle, stoop-shouldered man, and he didn't drink much. But in
the morning, for lunch, before dinner, and during the little
walk with the dog in the evening, he'd steal the glasses which
made life bearable for him. Day after day, year after year he
wet his whistle in this fashion. He gilded his days and hours
with the color of wine. Certainly Helvetia is a cheap land for
drinking, but even there you don't get far on two francs a day
when you want to slake your thirst. He needed about fifteen
Swiss francs to get through the day. In short: his modest
intemperance must be financed.

In his rumpled grayness he had nothing to sell in the way of either talent or charm. He had only his underpaid but highly confidential position in the Defense Department, with access to invaluable documents and likewise to the photocopy machines which were part of his daily employment as a copyist. No one found it strange to see him at the copy machine, even if it was on overtime. In truth he was as highly trusted as only a totally unimaginative, utterly obscure factotum can be. He was not a man who was above suspicion; he was *beneath* suspicion.

When he received his first offer from another country's embassy, he had already contracted debts of several hundred francs, and strictly speaking no longer had any choice. To ask for an advance was hopeless, and to tell his wife the truth was worse than death. The man stood on the brink of suicide. He accepted without haggling the shamelessly niggardly offer from the Soviet Embassy. They were well acquainted with his habits and his situation, his salary and his family life, and knew that there was no need to go high with him. He only needed enough for his small daily cups. Which he received. Everything was carefully planned out by his new employers; it was just a matter of copying certain documents and then leaving them behind in different places, always in new restaurants according to a system precisely worked out in relation to the days of the week. For him this meant no alteration in his habits, since he had long made it a practice to change drinking places so that no one should pick up the trail of his intemperance. He lived thus for nearly thirty years, and was finally discovered by pure accident. He received a whopping prison sentence, and did not protest.

During this time he procured documents of inestimable value for his brothers in the East, and instead of the millions he should have gotten for his investment, he received each month a sum of between four and five hundred francs for pocket money. Such was his life; thus can one treat a human being.

Once when Ali and I were on a trip in the desert, I told him the story. Ali's whole black face lit up, beaming with amusement.

"It's cheap to buy people," he replied. "Of all underpaid and trivial jobs, espionage is one of the worst-paying ones. The Russians especially are masters at turning the payment of their spies into pure blackmail. After all, you have a very good hold on a man who has delivered secret military documents to a foreign embassy. The only ones who earn money on espionage are publishers and movie producers. Almost all espionage goes on in the same sad, trivial way as with our little friend in Switzerland."

Ali is right; people can be very cheap. But it isn't their fault.

"You laugh at the story," I said to Ali, "and I could cry."

"What's the difference?" he replied.

Sometimes Ali and I drive out into the desert in his good old Fiat. We fill the car with provender and wine bottles and drive off; the nights we spend in this or that oasis, in this or that decaying hotel which tells us that the world is no longer the way it was in the old days, when the *jeunesse dorée* of every land, millionaires' wives and well-heeled consumptives, came there to take advantage of the healthy inland climate, of the warmth and the dry air—or just simply to die a death in beauty and, considering the luxury of the milieu, for a relatively reasonable sum. How cheap it can be to die.

The oases in this country are most reminiscent of the south slopes of the Swiss Alps, of Ticino—Tessin, with its high, dusty mountains and the palms from the last century, like a bad opera set from the romantic, dying, tuberculous nineties; it all looks as if it had been taken out of unaired wardrobes and bat-ridden flylofts. Everything is dark brownish-green and infested with spider webs. Moss grows on everything. Even the water in the *lago* is greenish-brown from gonorrhea and the past and a curious inclination to get the worst rains of the year right in the tourist season. The whole thing is like a Wagner opera at its most atrocious—a nature made of cardboard, papier-mâché, and painted canvas. In the pervasive twilight there's something brownish green about all the colors, if you can use such a word at all to describe this ersatz literary nature. Add to this an architecture which is unmatched anywhere on all this singular earth—a crematorium made manifest in imitation plaster, false patina, and warped Wagnerian wrought iron. Of course no other place in the world can be so dreadful as Tessin, and the oases too fall far short of it in topographical and architectonic horrors. The desert at least has truth. But they share the half-dead, moribund look of having once played a role during the bourgeoisie's last, soulful, and theatrical phase. The cities of the oasis retain nothing of their bygone varnish and gloss and facade; they are closer to reality. They look like rotting factory towns without the factories—a place where the walls are collapsing, not from external influences, but just from fatigue and hopelessness. They're simply moldering remains of clay and misery, sadder and more lonesome than anything else on earth. They don't have the same degree of falsehood as the Tessin cities, which are still pretending to be alive. They're openly poor, in contrast to their tuberculous sister cities in Switzerland—which are still trying to keep up the appearance of a sort of *pauvre honteux*. Tessin is like an old house, with gingerbread and scrollwork, which is still inhabited by three Italian sisters of good family; it's as if the old maids are still trying to make visitors think that they have money in the bank, and don't take just anyone under their roof as a paying guest.

This atmosphere no longer exists in the once world-famous oases. Here the decay is total. It's naked and it's true. One evening Ali and I stopped in one of the oases which, seventy or eighty years ago, were the most famous of all. I got out of the car and looked around me in the main street. Along one side, fifty to a hundred yards apart, stood three or four thin, withered little trees. There were hardly any people. On the other side a shabby palm tree bristled toward the sky in terror.

"There's the hotel," said Ali, pointing.

It was a tumbledown European building in the Tessin style, covered with ornaments and gingerbread, and with stucco sagging over the impoverished gray walls. There was no one to be seen on this side of the street either.

"Ali," I said, "both Gide and Wilde have been to this place. I must say that I'm amazed at how unperceptive their descriptions were. Neither of them connects it with Tessin."

"It was here that Gide met the Arab boy Achmed, who became his erotic ideal and ended up branding his libido for life."

"Ali, this is worse than Tessin, Capri, and Sorrento put together. So *this* is what Europe has left behind her in the desert!"

"No," said Ali, "it's worse than this. You don't know yet what the Europeans left behind them. Here there were once casinos and brothels, frolicsome Arab boys for a dollar apiece, everything consumptive whites could desire when looking for a suitable place to die. What you see is the ruins. It will take hundreds of years for you to comprehend what the Europeans have done in Africa."

"Shall I tell you a little about the conquest of Peru?" I said, "about how the great Francesco Pizarro made friends with the Incan emperor Atahualma, and managed to trick him into becoming the whites' prisoner?"

"No thanks. I know the story, but now we're in Africa, and what you haven't understood yet is that the whites have transformed the continent into one big European garbage can. We've even inherited their rats. Africa is one enormous European midden, a dump, a dungheap crawling with rats, excrement, and maggots. And it's worse in Equatorial Africa than here."

"I've been there."

"Have you seen Conakry?"

"Yes."

"Do you remember the smell?"

"Yes."

"Have you seen the marketplace? Do you remember the sound of the flies buzzing over the dark blue meat?"

"Why don't we talk about Wilde and Gide instead? Gide too came here because of tuberculosis, and then he found his Arab boy."

"It's okay with me," said Ali, "and don't forget that Gide was one of the first people to write the truth about Africa, long before it became the fashion among pinko European pseudo-intellectuals."

"Shut up!" I said.

"Look here," he went on, pointing: "Look what you've left behind: an empty and idioticized caricature of Europe. Look at the architecture, at the cornices, the gingerbread, and the eavestroughs! Eavestroughs in the desert! The whole thing is a caricature of Europe. Do you remember the government buildings in Conakry?"

"Yes, yes, yes!!!" I shouted. "I remember the stucco and the gewgaws and the garden sculptures and the dreadful churchyards and the whole French culture like excrement from Europe. BUT EUROPE HAS STILL HAD ENORMOUS CULTURAL AND SCIENTIFIC CREATIVE POWER!"

Ali laughed his golden, bubbling Negro laughter.

"It's so easy to lure you people out of your good white skin. You have such a thin veneer over your barbarism that it only costs me a few words to bring the cave man out into the daylight."

"You should talk!" I said. "You who are just a waste product of Europe! You're so sure of yourself because you have a couple of shitty French doctor's degrees and speak three or four European languages. All your self-confidence comes from the fact that you know more about Europe than the Europeans do themselves. But is that any standard for the Africans? You judge each other by how far you've succeeded in imitating *us*."

"Go on!"

In front of the hotel stood three youngish men. All were dressed in the foolish and impractical European suits—with tight sleeves, buttoned-up jackets, and long trousers, which would hold the heat in next to the body.

"You don't even dare use your own clothes. To be regarded as human by other Africans, you have to get yourselves up in this nonsense. It's only when you're posing for a color photo by that dirt-poor national travel bureau of yours that you get someone to help you dress up in burnooses and slippers and whatchamacallits and pose you beside some old relic of an arteriosclerotic camel, so that the state can make colored tourist brochures of you and try to lure some half-mad European or schizophrenic American to this country to leave a little hard currency. You've never had any other yard-stick than hard currency."

"No," said Ali, "only you have that."

We both began to laugh, and after carefully locking the car we went across the street and into the hotel bar. It was shady, cool, and quiet.

"A triple gin with bitters and tonic for my European friend," I said, nodding toward Ali's ebony head. The bar-tender immediately started laughing, and Ali went on:

"And a glass of lemonade for our little *sal arabe!*"

The Arab behind the bar laughed harder and harder, and half an hour later we were both a little drunk.

Life was livable.

We started talking about The Nice American, and how we didn't know how he was getting along after what happened two or three weeks ago. Neither of us had any idea whether he had survived or not. The Nice American had hardly any acquaintances other than Ali and me; so it must be just the hospital staff and the authorities who were looking after him now; whether he got well again or not, he would be sent home in a well-packaged condition.

It was I who discovered The Nice American, and it wasn't out here in the desert (even though it could well have been, which would have been better for all concerned)—it was in the fish restaurant next to the mosque.

I was sitting there one evening, and over at the bar I saw a man—or more precisely, a man's back. This back, which was unusually large, looked as if it belonged to a giant, and the head sitting on the shoulders was light yellow like corn above the red, sunburned neck. He was enormously blond and just

as enormously large. And there was something the matter
with him. When he got up—that is, tried to get up—it was
easy to see what ailed him: he was almost dead drunk. He
could just barely stay on his feet. Beside him stood a prostitute, a black girl.

She was no special delight to look at, rather fat and about
half-drunk, and didn't seem particularly intelligent either. But
he was genuinely taken with her, and they were using a kind
of sign language between themselves. The simplest and clear-
est sign consisted in her holding her glass up in front of him
and showing him that it was empty. After that she pointed to
the wall of bottles in the background, and again into the glass
to show how it could be filled again. Thus they were sitting
and talking together.

The conversation was neither complicated nor interesting,
but it kept evoking more laughter in them both; and certain
things indicated that they would like to touch on deeper subjects, but since she didn't speak a word of English and he
didn't understand a syllable of her language, the possibilities
for verbal communication were extremely slight. To break
the ice, he held his left hand up to her and made a ring with
his thumb and forefinger, then stuck the index finger of his
right hand into the hole between the fingers and moved it
back and forth, in and out, again and again. She gave a howl
of delight, and all the Arabs at the bar began to laugh out
loud. He looked up, rather surprised, but smiled amiably
when he realized that they had all understood what he
wanted. And it is good for a human being to be understood.

He said a few more words to her, but they were obviously
in English, for she shook her head in incomprehension. So he
turned toward the restaurant and, looking out over the tables,
caught sight of me and a few other guests. After a brief delib-
eration, he decided to cast himself out into the unknown, and
let go of the bar. Now he was in high sea; nothing daunted,
he met the waves like an old caravel. He rolled violently in
the swells, tossing from side to side, but did not capsize. With
the wind slightly abaft the beam he headed northwest

through the room; he grazed a couple of vacant tables, but didn't run aground. Once he was in smooth waters, he grabbed the back of a chair and dropped anchor in front of an elderly French lady.

Having ascertained by repeated hailings that she didn't speak English, he weighed anchor anew and set out before a stiff breeze. Again he avoided running aground, came about, and headed under full sail directly for two native business-men. He tried to back nicely in front of them, but still took the pier with considerable force. There was no need to hail them, for they explained instantly—partly in French and partly by signs—that they didn't understand English. Now he spied out over the whole room, sighted me and cast off. With the wind off the starboard quarter he took the waves with rel-ative ease, and, though he heeled strongly a couple of times, reached an emergency port at my table and anchored on the roadstead—in this case the straight-backed chair right across from me. Then he made fast.

For awhile he just sat looking at me benignly, nodding slightly and mopping his forehead with his handkerchief. Then he said:

"You speak English?"

"Yes," I said, and here our acquaintance began.

He turned around and waved to the black girl, who came over to our table and sat down, after introducing herself to me politely. It was then my task to function as interpreter.

"What are you drinking?" asked The Nice American: "Whiskey?"

She asked for vermouth, and every time I saw her after-wards she always wanted vermouth. Perhaps she had stomach pains, or was suffering from a common occupational disease for people in her line of work, as well as for night-club girls— a chronic alcohol poisoning which leads to intestinal catarrh. At any rate, she drank vermouth.

The Nice American invited her home with him for the night, and she replied that she would gladly come—but another time, when he wasn't so drunk as now. He understood, and didn't try to coax her further.

"He's been asking me all evening," she told me. "Why is he so insistent? Surely he's too drunk to have any real need?"

"For white Americans it's a great refinement to go to bed with blacks; it means breaking all taboos," I explained.

"What the Sham Hill are you shitting there talking about?" he asked.

"She wants to know why you, as an American, have come to a revolutionary country," I said. "What are you doing here?"

"I'm a petroleum specialist," he replied. "I work out there in the desert. I'm only visiting this city for a few days. I help them process the oil."

"Are you a communist?" I asked. "Or just a sympathizer?"

"Nothing! I'm absolutely nothing."

His diction was quite indistinct now, and he repeated: "Nothing!"

He took the black prostitute's hand, and sat there patting it for a long time while he tried to make eye contact with her. She asked for another vermouth, and he ordered a double-double-double whiskey for himself. It proved to be his last, and it hit him amidships. You might say he was shipping water from all directions—but gradually righted himself, with a decided list to port. Before things got that far, though, he had managed to explain why he was living and working in this country:

"I'm from Texas," he said, with a strange, enigmatic expression, as if the explanations of all the earth's mysteries lay buried in that one little piece of information.

"Okay," I said: "So?"

"Back there we know about oil."

"But why are you here?"

"They pay so darn well here. Damn well."

"You didn't get tired of Texas, then?"

"Fuck Texas!"

I saw that he was missing two fingers on his left hand.

"Have you had an accident?" I asked, pointing to his hand.

"They're back in Vietnam," he replied. "It's just pure luck that my balls aren't back there too. My whole corpse, for that matter. Fuck Nixon!"

He sat there for awhile staring at his hand, as if this were the first time he'd really noticed the missing fingers. After a bit he looked up at me, almost pleading:

"Can't you talk her into coming home with me tonight?"

"It's no use. She said no. And I know that no prostitute likes to sleep with drunks—it takes them so long to make it. It's wearing for the girl."

"Try once more anyway!"

I translated it for her, and she repeated—very firmly—what she had said before: She could come when he'd sobered up.

"I'll never be sober again," he said, "not if I can help it. Translate that for her!"

I did, and she asked for a vermouth. He pulled a roll of bills out of his pocket, looked at it confusedly for awhile, pocketed it again—then called for the vermouth. His own whiskey was only half gone. Just then came the gust which almost overturned him. From now on he hung over the rail like a wet rag; all his rigging threatened to sink into the sea. There was nothing to do but get him home. I got the name of his hotel out of him and decided to take him there. Soon I had paid for both of us, and helped him to the door. We came out into the darkness of the street, and I set our course up toward one of the main thoroughfares to get a taxi.

Immediately a wild yell rang from the street, and the young beggars were upon us. He flung out a handful of coins, and the yells grew wilder. A couple of the children tried to reach into his pockets, but I chased them away. And more had arrived—it was indeed a disquietingly large flock of children, maybe close to fifty of them now. The Nice American threw them more coins and then some bills, which predictably made the situation worse. They grabbed at his jacket and pant legs, forced their thin fingers down into his pockets, and placed themselves menacingly in our way. I was forced to swat them away from him, the way you chase off insects, and soon it took all my strength to get him out of there. But the children didn't give up; they followed us howling like lunatics, blocked our way and tried to stop us. Most of them pursued us all the way up to the Avenue Che Guevara, where I managed to hail a taxi. I stuffed him into the back seat and crawled in after him. At the hotel I had to help him up to his room and put him to bed.

Such was my first meeting with our Nice American. In all, I saw him only a few more times.

He wasn't always so drunk, and we liked to sit and talk when we met. Gradually both Ali and I learned to think very highly of him. He was really a good-hearted fellow.

It was also true that he'd fought in Indochina, and he's the first honest eyewitness I've talked with. He thought that the war was due to big undersea oil deposits off the south coast of Indochina, oil which is far more valuable than the other raw materials the United States can procure from that part of Asia.

"You're an oil specialist," I replied, "and you see oil everywhere."

"No," he said, "the oil is real enough. But the finds have been kept secret for many years. Everybody is after oil. Look where the disturbances are—and you'll see that the oil isn't far away. It's in the neighborhood. The Middle East: oil. Biafra: oil. And the most hellish place God has created on earth: Texas! It has a drop or two of oil too. You could write a history of fossil oil, and it would coincide with the rest of military history. Fuck the petroleum!"

It sometimes seemed as if he had oil on the brain; he had gradually developed a whole philosophy of oil. Everything having to do with politics and violence and war was to him directly or indirectly related to one mineral, oil. Oil was the blood of the globe. It caused greater misfortunes than gold had ever brought us. Practically all the wretchedness, misery, and unhappiness which humankind had to endure came from oil. The reason he was working in this country was not just the high salaries which a technologically underdeveloped land must pay for imported expertise; in reality he was waging his own little oil war based on the assumption that strengthening the position of the small and middle-sized oil powers would weaken that of the superpowers in the fight for oil.

"It's just like I said," he explained. "I'm not a communist, but I'm anti-superpower. That's why I've gone in for helping to destroy the American oil monopolies. The more the small and middle-sized oil-producing nations can refine their own oil, the stronger they'll be on the world market—and the Americans, the Russians, and Europe will be correspondingly weaker. Of course it's not much I can do, but it's something. And whatever expertise I have is at the disposal of the looted countries which are now standing up to the parasites."

Of course he was a communist, but he didn't want to admit it, because he felt more virginal without a political label.

"Once in a while, " he said, "I see the globe in front of me as one big map of oil deposits. It's like there's oil trickling out all over. The whole world is spun into a fine, branching net of oil veins, the way a human body has blood vessels. It's something like the stream of gold that flows between stock exchanges and banks and big businesses all over the world, but I think the oil is more real than the money. At one time gold—money—was the curse of the earth, but today everything revolves around oil. It's in oil that the Prince of Darkness reveals himself today, the guy we called Satan in the good old days. When they've definitely abandoned gold as a monetary standard, they ought to go over to the oil standard—print on the bills that they can be redeemed at such and such a national bank for so many ounces of oil. Oil has the further advantage over gold that it can be *used.* You can easily carry on a war without gold, but not without oil. When you come right down to it, gold is nothing but a symbol anyway; you can't run a tank on gold, but you can run both tanks and bombers on oil. And actually it's war that decides everything; today we have no other standard. Might makes right, and might is oil. Every time I see jet planes, fighter planes, bombers, anything, I get a quiet pleasure out of thinking that without oil these monsters aren't worth the air they pollute. They're dead and useless without this oil which comes up out of the ground. Today all real politics is a battle for oil."

Sometimes The Nice American was so drunk that we had to carry him home, and every evening the battle with the children was hell to get through. It was obvious that all the children knew him and his largesse, and they thronged in quite astonishing numbers to get hold of some of the money he strewed around. We often had to use harsh measures to get past them, and they responded with shouts of hate, and sometimes by throwing stones.

Now that he was staying more sober, he had also been allowed to enjoy the favors of the black girl; she sometimes went to the hotel with him and stayed the night. He paid her very well, but made no progress in French. Out in the desert where the oil is, he got along very well with no language but English, so he didn't need another. At the restaurant he was very popular, and was always treated most cordially. They would also get him a taxi when he needed it to get back to the hotel.

Actually Ali knew him better than I did, and the two of them would often drink and talk together the whole evening. The American usually did most of the talking, while Ali listened—probably because Ali had found an expert on things about which he himself knew nothing, and from whom Ali, with his unquenchable thirst for knowledge, could suck new information. Perhaps he reckoned that at some future time he might find something to do with oil in his own country. This year new oil finds were spreading like wildfire all over the world; why should the black part of Africa be the only place without oil wells? Certainly Ali had his plans about this as about everything else, but I think that there was also a kind of real friendship between the two, or at least a genuine sympathy.

But often The Nice American was alone in the restaurant down by the fish market, and he always got drunkest when he was lonely—for all I know he may have been homesick, for Indochina or Texas or God knows where. At any rate, he got drunk.

And so finally it happened, the thing which put a stop to the association among the three of us, and also between him and the black girl. As he so often did, he had sat there till past midnight, and in the course of the evening had drunk a great deal, and in an unguarded moment decided to walk home alone.

What the children had done to him nobody knows exactly, but farther up toward the main streets they had pushed him into a dark alley, where the fleecing and the mauling had then taken place. As always, of course, they had been standing outside the restaurant begging for small change and bread, and when he came out they had, as usual, begged as much as possible from him; and when they understood that he really was alone, they had jumped him, torn off his clothes and abused him with kicks and blows, and probably clubbed him as well. He was found the next morning, still unconscious. The children had also used knives to cut and stab him with, and had cut him up especially around the eyes and sex organs. A couple of the biggest boys in the flock had probably enjoyed him sexually as well.

So afterwards the police had great difficulty identifying his bloody and half-dead remains.

Neither Ali nor I knew whether he had survived the onslaught or whether he had died from it.

The police had visited all the nearby restaurants in an effort to identify the victim, and it was Achmed who had told them about the two missing fingers on the left hand. Then they knew who he was, and where he came from.

Now it belongs in the story that this isn't the first time an adult has been assaulted and beaten up or killed by such flocks of children. When they attack, maybe twenty or thirty of them at once, with all the savagery and all the rage which is usually confined to their horrible yells, even an uncommonly strong man won't have a chance against them if he's alone.

It may be that such starving and half-wild bands of children are a part of every revolution—or rather, are an effect of
the conditions which have provoked the revolution, but
which are not yet conquered or relegated to the past. In
Russia they had the same wild bands of children for years
after the revolution—starving, frozen, and hostile, permeated
with hatred for all adults. So we have something similar here,
in the form of the howling children outside our restaurants.
"Byezprizorni" they called them in Russia; here we don't have
any special name for them. They're just here as a matter of
course; when you've been here awhile you no longer notice
them any more than you notice the excrement in the street or
the swarms of flies around it. But they roam all over near the
harbor and the main streets, like incarnations of hatred for all
who have helped to make this world the way it is. They themselves are the excrement of society.

Ali and I were sitting in the bar of the hotel in the old,
decaying luxury town, the once world-famous oasis. We had
both drunk quite a bit, but were still clear-headed.

We were talking about our friend—indeed already a dear
one—The Nice American; but now we called him Samuel,
which was his real name. "The only way to get rid of these
starving bands of children is to carry through the permanent
revolution," said Ali.

"We don't have them in Northern Europe," I replied.

"No, but Northern Europe isn't Africa or India or Latin
America—and it's there that the battle is going on today.
You're so European that you can't even imagine anything
decisive happening outside Europe or North America. But I
tell you that today everything which means most for the
future is happening in Asia, Africa, and South America. You
don't believe it, because your thinking is by nature
Eurocentric, if I can use such a word as 'thinking' in this connection. You quite simply don't *feel* it as a reality.

"And this is the point: Samuel had learned his lesson—he
knew that the things which have been done in the Orient are
now coming home with manifold intensity."

"What do you mean?"

"I mean that you regard *reality* as something which is only found in Europe or in North America. Has Samuel told you much about his glorious campaign in Indochina?"

"No, nothing."

"That was mostly what we sat and talked about when we were alone. He'd seen more than was good for him, more than he could stand to see."

"How's that?"

"Well, I'll tell you a few of the things you don't know about him, and which are more important than his oil philosophy.

"In the first place Samuel was a deserter. He not only deserted, but he went straight over to the enemy. There were reasons for this. That is: there were very good reasons, but one in particular. He had a definite, perfectly splendid reason for going over to the enemy. This unusually excellent reason was that he hadn't asked permission to take part in this war over there. A further reason, of course, was that this kind of war—a partisan war, guerilla war, rebellion, civil war, revolution or the like—always turns more bestial than do normal, so to speak bourgeois wars, because in this kind of extraordinary campaign you're always fighting against a hidden enemy— you're fighting against conspiracies and invisible resistance movements, and therefore atrocities are a part of the war's very methodology. Every time you take a prisoner, you have a chance of coming across secrets of military value. Besides, everyone is a potential spy, and the whole civilian population are potential resistance fighters who may be working closely with the enemy. Every prisoner you take, every peasant you see, and every child, every woman, and every old person may chance to be in possession of information. Torture of prisoners thus becomes a matter of daily routine. You know how it was in this country before the master race, after several years of civil war, was forced to give up and go back home to the leprous Europe they came from.

"It was like that over there too. The only difference was in the terrain. There was much more forest and jungle than here.

"In short: Samuel didn't like his job.

"So one day he took off and went straight over to the enemy—which was very dangerous, because he had to pass scouts and firing lines to get there.

"In one way or another he ended up in a tranquil little village on the other side, where he lived in peace and harmony with the villagers, who soon learned to value his good-hearted disposition. He was already a nice American back then. Of course Samuel's enormous height was also a strange addition to the life of the village—he was almost twice as tall as most of his former enemies. And people would often come from other villages just to look at him. They gave him food and valued him highly. In return he turned out to be a genius at carrying water and wood—but above all he could instruct the villagers in the art of taking cover during the American bombing raids. He knew from experience how the Americans attacked, and he also had a much better psychological understanding of the nature of American warfare than the natives did—so to some extent he could predict the attacks, and thus be of real help to this remarkably friendly population. His fame spread through the jungle, and one day a group of the former enemy's soldiers came to look him over. As a gift they brought some liquor, which he hadn't seen since he changed sides, and Samuel almost cried at the sight of the gift. Both the small soldiers and the village's inhabitants stood around him in a respectful but most friendly circle while he emptied the bottle in three or four gulps. They invited him along to headquarters and he went with them, clad in pajamas which were much too small and a flat straw hat which the women had made for him in a suitable size. They cried when he left, but both the soldiers and he himself assured them that he would return very soon.

"He stayed in the enemy quarters for awhile, and he told them all he knew about American tactics and technology, their way of thinking strategically, their mental peculiarities; what scared them, how they advanced, and what they expected the enemy to react to. At this point Samuel was an experienced, much-decorated soldier; there's no doubt whatever that he made himself very useful to the Asians before he returned to his life in the village.

"Among the peasants all was as before, and nothing bad would have happened had the village not been visited by the whites, who suspected it of harboring enemy forces. The natives were able to give timely warning to the only one they harbored, Samuel, who went off and hid in the forest. But he didn't go so far away that he couldn't keep track of what was happening to the villagers. Unfortunately everything that could happen did.

"The whites undertook a punitive expedition, and they did everything they usually did on such occasions, from raping all the younger women to disemboweling them with bayonets. They tied the natives together with barbed wire and pulled them out one by one—for interrogation, as they call it. It developed into an orgy in the art of educating the civilian population to obedience. Moreover, the soldiers were well provided with booze, as well as other substances which can impart courage to tired warriors.

"What Samuel now witnessed was in principle nothing new to him; it was all familiar from before. But this time it was happening to his close friends in the village, to people who had taken care of him, and whom he loved. He knew every single one of them, and saw most of them die a choice and protracted death, except for older women and small children, who for the most part were just herded together and shot down with machine guns. Of course they screamed horribly.

"It's necessary to go through all these things in detail—otherwise it will be hard to understand Samuel's reaction. It was powerful.

"We can treat the whole thing quite generally; we may just as well make a list of the purely routine practices. First I'll take the interrogation methods, in order of frequency when it comes to the handling of prisoners:

"1) Elementary physical abuse—blows with fists or with objects, with rifle butts and other things—including, of course, kicks in the belly, solar plexus and crotch. One of the most-used forms was to tie the prisoner's feet together and take off his shoes and then hit him with a stick or a gun butt on the soles of his feet. It doesn't sound so bloody, but causes unbearable pain. When it's a matter of getting people to talk, the procedure isn't bad. But still it's just the first degree of interrogation. If the prisoner refuses to talk—or if he has nothing to tell—he's taken further.

"2) The bamboo method, which is harsher, presupposes that you're sojourning in a country where bamboo is always on hand. You split the bamboo cane and sharpen the splinters into a point at one end. These can be used in different ways; for example you can stick them into the prisoner's ears and pound them further and further in through the eardrums, until both ears are punctured. Then you can use somewhat smaller splinters to stick under the prisoners' nails and little by little drive them so far in that they come between the nails and the finger bones. If you keep it up, the bamboo spikes will eventually come out again at the joints where the fingers go over into the hand. In each prisoner you have ten fingers to do this with. If that doesn't help, you do the same thing with the toes. You can also stick bamboo splinters through all the soft parts of the body, in the armholes, in the stomach— through the breasts of women prisoners, into the abdominal cavity—or you can sharpen a thick bamboo stick and drive it into the vagina in women or the rectum in men. This reminds me that in the country where we are now, the master race was a nation of great wine drinkers, and instead of bamboo sticks they used wine bottles in the same fashion—that is, to pound into the natural openings of the prisoners who were being interrogated.

"3) There are also other things you can do with the fingers: cut them loose with knives or snip them off with wire cutters, joint by joint. You can first use electric pliers to pull out the nails with if desired. There are also nails on the toes.

"4) The procedures which are still more or less natural include the methods with wet leather thongs, which are bound around the neck and the ankles, with the legs bent up backwards as far as possible, i.e. toward the subject's back. When the thongs begin to dry, they shrink, and the prisoner is slowly strangled or his back is broken at a very slow tempo.

"5) Now we encounter the technical methods: first, what you can do with an ordinary car battery. You make a sort of leather belt, lined on the inside with metal wires—and you just hook these wires up to a standard 12-volt battery. It works wonders, even on the least cooperative prisoner. The point here is not electric shock—just the warming effect of the current. The wires get red-hot and leave stripes where the belts have been applied.

"6) Then there's the water method: You stuff the prisoner's mouth with a big wet cloth, and then you stick a rubber hose into his or her nostrils, and put a funnel into the other end of the hose. Then you pour in water, and in this way the prisoner can be kept on the edge of drowning for hours. The method reached its high point in this country, where the colonial masters combined it with inserting a garden hose into the rectum of the person to be interrogated, so that his whole belly swelled up to an astonishing size. It was very effective, but had the drawback that in many prisoners it led to a rupture of the intestinal wall, so that they died of peritonitis a while after the interrogation.

"7) The telephone method is well-known, and need only be mentioned briefly, despite its many positive sides. As you know, it leaves almost no marks, or only very small burns where the electrodes have been attached. You use a simple, ordinary field telephone, and this is one of the other advantages of the method. Then you can fasten the electrodes where you like—for example, one in each ear, so that the relatively high voltage goes straight through the head. An important point is that while the tension is high, the amperage is low, which means that you can keep it up with a prisoner almost indefinitely. The painful effect is absolutely amazing, and this is the objective: the worst possible pain combined with the least possible danger to life.

"Where to place the electrodes is up to the interrogator's imagination, but the most common place is in the sex organs, perhaps in the rectum and the penis, or the penis and the nostrils, inside the urethra and in the tongue (to which the conductor is often fastened by sticking it through the tongue)—and on women you can also fasten the conductors to the nipples and inside the vagina. Here there are no limits for the clever and inventive.

"8) The helicopter methods can be varied. The simplest is to take three or four prisoners up with you and throw out a couple of them if they refuse to give candid answers to your questions. Then those who are left will often be more compliant than they were down on land. Another procedure is to take one of the prisoners up between two helicopters—that is, tied with one line to each machine. As soon as you're up in the air, the helicopters move slowly apart, while the subject is torn in two. That also softens up the other prisoners.

"A third method is to tie a rope around the ankle of a prisoner and let him dangle under the machine while you fly so low that he's dragged through the treetops. They lose a good deal of skin in this way, especially if you set the speed up a bit. You can also let the prisoner down on two ropes—with one, the longer, around the chest, and the other, shorter rope around his neck. When you slowly ease him down, he'll feel the rope around his neck tighten first, and you let him hang like that while the other prisoners watch.

"9) A related procedure is to let one or two gooks be dragged after a jeep down a hill. But these things are dependent on internal combustion engines.

"10) Of course they have special methods of treating women. And the soldiers are instructed in them before they're sent into action. First and foremost you have your bamboo to stick through the softest parts of the female body, such as the breasts, the rump, the armpits, and the outer part of the sex organs—or high up in the interior of the abdomen. But one of the most common things is that first of all the female prisoner is made the object of a gang rape—let's say she's tied with her feet apart and then raped by a whole company. This is already rather effective, but it has its limit at the point where the prisoner loses consciousness. In general the methods of interrogating women have a strongly sexual character—it's not uncommon, for instance, to make a fire and heat up a bayonet until it's red-hot, and then stick the glowing bayonet up into the prisoner's uterus. Another form of amusement is to stick the most varied things up into the bellies of those who are uncooperative, for example filling the vagina with phosphorus or corrosive liquids and then sewing the opening together with wire. Grenades or small flares are also often stuck up in the vagina and allowed to explode, so that the belly is blown up or torn to pieces. But in this field private initiative is utterly without restrictions or limits. The cleverest get furthest.

"11) Now we pass beyond the concept of interrogation techniques, to more general massacres, where everything is obliterated; houses burned or bombed out, the populace gathered and killed with machine guns: men, old people, women, children, and in addition water buffaloes, sheep, goats, chickens—and on to the crops in the fields. The massacres are done thoroughly, and those who aren't mown down are only set aside temporarily to be interrogated before they're killed.

"They go thoroughly to work on old women and children, because experience has shown that these very often have weapons concealed on them. Children are often dispatched by being given so-called 'cookies'—poisoned tablets which are fatal when eaten. But on such occasions no prisoners are taken; all are exterminated.

"12) As the last point we must mention the whites' strange collection mania: parts of native corpses. This is very characteristic and has nothing to do with any utilitarian considerations of military technology. They simply collect cut-off fingers or ears from the dead, and may also collect severed sex organs. There are people who collect whole chopped-off heads. The severed heads are of course relatively large and difficult to carry from place to place, so most people content themselves with ears, fingers, breasts, penises and the outer parts of the vagina—and they often carry along jelly glasses for preserving these parts of the body in alcohol. Hand in hand with this goes the simple maiming of the corpses, done not with an eye to collecting, but purely for the sake of enjoyment.

"As you see: It wasn't just in the good old colony times that the whites spread civilization and culture among the inferior races—they're still doing it. The whites' culture is being disseminated day by day in every part of the world.

"I just mention this so that you'll understand why Samuel reacted so strongly when he saw his village being visited by his white countrymen from the land of Indians and oil. I don't know exactly what the soldiers did beyond the purely routine while they were wiping out this little village where he had been so kindly and warmly treated—but it resulted in Samuel's leaving his hiding place and going straight into the village square, which now lay strewn with his dead friends. One of the NCO's was just in the act of dispatching the last of the children when Samuel, something over six foot six, arrived on the scene arrayed in slippers, mini-pajamas, and a straw hat. It belongs to the story that at this point he was dreaming of being able to adopt a couple of children from this part of the world.

"He went straight up to the sergeant and laid his hand in front of the machine-gun barrel, with the result that out of simple astonishment the man pressed the trigger again, something which cost Samuel two fingers. With the other hand he knocked the noncom to the ground, where he lay for a long time. When Samuel first appeared, the other whites stood just as petrified as if they had met a ghost; but after the sergeant had been knocked out, they came to their senses again. Samuel was overpowered, loudly proclaiming all the while what he thought of them and the President and the war.

"His countrymen didn't doubt for a moment that he was a howling, raving maniac. Therefore nothing bad happened to him, except that he was led away in chains and subsequently sent by helicopter to the nearest madhouse.

"Later he was sent home to good old Texas, where he no

longer felt at home, and after finishing his education in the oil line he came over here. He's been here ever since, and so today he's lying, alive or dead, in the hospital."

Later—when we got back from our trip in the desert—we met again to eat supper at the fish restaurant. We arrived before the usual time, so the children hadn't yet laid siege to the exit.

Achmed came quietly over to us; he already had the bottles of wine.

"Anything new?" asked Ali.

"No," he replied at first, but then quickly added: "*Le gentil americain* is dead. The police were here and notified us."

We ate shrimp.

Pizarro was over fifty years old and could not yet read or write. He was originally a foundling, the bastard offspring of parents in the province of Estramadura. He grew up as a swineherd among strangers, and all his life he continued to feel inferior because he couldn't sign his name. On the other hand, he had no bent for bookish pursuits either, and never tried to decipher the alphabet.

Later he journeyed to America in search of treasure, but he did not succeed at first.

At fifty, as I said, he was living in Panama—and he felt that his days were running out like grains of sand in an hourglass; his life was burning down like a wax candle before the Holy Virgin.

The great Pizarro made three journeys.

The first was in search of gold. He found the gold, and became convinced that he had found an unknown but great and mighty kingdom. This was Peru.

The second was in search of more gold. He obtained more gold, but above all he spied out the Incas' enormous land.

The third was in search of the rest of the gold, and to conquer the land—because he had found it, and because the land was treasure trove, so to speak, and consequently belonged to him and to the Spanish Crown.

When the last journey began Pizarro was sixty years old, and his relationship to the art of reading and writing was just as platonic as ever. On the other hand, he could do arithmetic.

The appropriation of others' property he regarded as neither theft, pillage, rapine, nor grave-robbing, but as his manifest right. His carnivore blood never forsook the swineherd from Estramadura.

Once, then, there lay a mighty kingdom by the shore of a great, great sea. This land was not yet discovered by men, but only by the Indians. These *indios* had been dwelling on this coast for twelve thousand years when the whites came. And twelve thousand years is a long time to go around waiting to be discovered. Therefore both the Incas and the other inhabitants of the land of Peru were very happy when the first white man came sailing to their shores, and they received him with great friendliness. They gave him large gifts of gold and precious stones, and both the man himself—who was called Pizarro—and his crew and his soldiers rejoiced greatly over the gifts, and in the secret chambers of their hearts resolved to return as soon as possible in order to appropriate to themselves the kingdom and all its treasures, and to convert the redskins to the Lord of Sabaoth and bring them under the rule of the Pope and their Catholic Spanish Majesties—so that their red souls, along with their red gold and precious gems, should not incur eternal torments in the hereafter, but should henceforth be assured a place, albeit a modest one, in the Kingdom of Heaven.

No sooner thought than done.

The kingdom of Peru was governed by the Incas through a huge bureaucracy as a perfect communist state. The government commanded enormous riches, and the country was more highly organized socially than any other state known to history. Poverty and unemployment, hunger and money were unknown concepts. No one profited from others' toil; everyone received the necessities of food and clothing from government depots. The disabled and the aged were treated the same as those who worked. This Peruvian empire was the world's first welfare state.

One ill-fated day in the year of wrath 1531 Pizarro arrived, with three ships, in the capacity of Peru's newly appointed governor. At about this time his more humane and considerate colleague Cortez had discovered a heathen Indian tribe in the present Florida, and had chastised the tribe for its unbelief by cutting off the lips and noses of the assembled populace, along with the breasts of the women—so that in the future they should serve the Lord Jehovah and grasp the message of love given by the carpenter's son. The witnesses reported that all this nose- and lip-cutting gave rise to a painfully loud wailing and a prodigious quantity of blood. Not least were the women and children said to have screamed horribly, occasioning great merriment among the Christians—as did the thusly chastised Indians' baptism and initiation into the community of the Lamb.

With Pizarro, in Peru, things proceeded in a more lively fashion, especially after he had understood in earnest what riches were in the custody of the rather unwarlike heathens who had hitherto administered the country. In Lima the houses were actually partly of gold, of pure and genuine, heavy gold—which now belonged to the highly Christian Majesties of the kingdom of Spain, as well as to the Holy See in Rome.

There is no reason to go into more detail, but a few aspects of the case deserve attention nonetheless—if only because they follow the line which shows our brother humans' ways and wanderings on the earth, and can thereby contribute to our forming a correct and not illusory picture of the dubious but advanced animal species to which we belong. We are confronted, for example, with extremely striking parallels between the fates of Mexico and Peru. Before the white two-legged saviors appeared on the scene, there existed in both countries an ancient prophecy that when the white gods came over the sea, the days of the kingdom would be numbered; decline would accompany the armor-clad men with the firearms. Both in Peru and in Mexico there arose simultaneously with the whites' arrival an internal political dissolution, leading to divisions and civil strife. Furthermore, in both countries the whites, with the aid of treachery and deceit, succeeded in taking the emperor of the realm as prisoner. And in both countries the emperors were killed. Montezuma was stoned, his successor hanged. Things took a less humane course in Peru: the emperor was originally to have been roasted in Christian fashion, but at the sight of the flames he gave in and declared his willingness to receive the faith of the conquerors. This resulted in his being given a wooden cross between his fettered hands and feet, after which he was decently baptized and piously executed by garotte.

But otherwise Pizarro and his priests made use primarily of the stake. One chief after another was burned, but always after due process of law—for example on a charge of pederasty, sodomy, or fornication, or for heresy and unbelief.

A great many others were flayed alive, especially those who couldn't work diligently enough in the mines to provide the Church and the king with sufficient gold. Today, of course, we have no figures on those who were so justly executed, but it can be said that a great nation was almost exterminated. At the same time we must also realize that men like Cortez and Pizarro were by no means hypocrites using the Church as a pretext for enriching themselves; the truth is that both were pious, believing, deeply Christian men.

The work in the mines likewise gave rise to a need for meting out punishments to the always lazy and ungrateful Indians. And today we still have a fine selection of graphic sheets which show us the chastisement and disciplining of the indolent natives. But considering what heights pictorial art back home in Europe had reached at this point—I need only mention Toscana and Quattrocento, plus names such as Fra Angelico, Giotto, Cimabue, and many, many more—these historically important but primitively executed drawings from the colonies are without aesthetic value.

They were simple but brave and courageous men who conquered those distant lands, not folk weighed down by learning or other inhibitions of the human spirit. At this time both Sandro Botticelli and Hieronymous Bosch had passed away; on the other hand, Benvenuto Cellini was still a young man. Calvin reigned in Geneva, Albrecht Dürer had just died in Germany. The witches' bonfires flamed lustily all over Europe—the continent which the Lord has chosen to receive the only true religion on earth.

It was a beautiful, sun-gold morning when Pizarro and his steel-clad men first beheld the emperor of the Incas. And it was high, high up in the mountains—so high that the whites were already gasping for breath, their hearts pounding, because of the thin air. This was after a long and almost fatal march through Peru—up into ever higher mountains, through ever narrower passes, scaling ever steeper cliffs. The Indians had a much slower pulse, and suffered not at all from the low air pressure. Despite the mountain air they could sprint for days on end, born runners that they were.

Their progression to the Emperor Atahualpa's mountain home had been written in blood and flame, and everywhere the Christians had been victorious. It was the Indians who were burned. By treachery and guile the whites succeeded in meeting the emperor of the Incas; they presented him with a Bible, and when he showed no visible delight in the gift, they took him prisoner. They had already lured him into ambush. He had almost no entourage, and could not defend himself against the steel-clad men with the firearms.

As a punishment for Atahualpa's having thus scorned the Bible and the Word of God, they decided to burn him alive. After all, why the deuce should he die a more comfortable death than other prisoners?

But—as indicated above—he let himself be converted to Christianity when he saw the flames rising from the stake. As a reward for his having sought God's grace on his deathbed, he was just slowly strangled instead. Actually, Atahualpa escaped very cheaply from his meeting with the whites; it cost him no more than his life and his imperial throne. Soon the kingdom went into dissolution. Yet another culture had been killed.

The illiterate Pizarro had fulfilled the destiny which God had assigned him; his work was done. Peru was in ruins. Later he himself died a most involuntary death—slain by one of his own European fellow butchers.

I walk these streets thinking about the violent destructive power which has emanated from Europe. Colonial history is like a sponge saturated with blood! Take hold of it, and it drips—and the drops are red.

To write the history of Peru is to write the history of colonialism; first come the soldiers, then come the priests, then come the ravens and the jackals. Then banks and corporations are founded, for we shall inherit the earth in all its glory.

No matter where you look, you find the same faces, the same deeds, the same spirit. Through the fair kingdoms of earth we march to Paradise with singing. We have made the injustice into a shrine.

Let us take a picture from the sporting Englishmen's regime in India; the Britons have always been admired for their inborn sense of fair play. This is taken from the *Times* in the last century:

> Some of the sepoys were still breathing. They were dispatched—it was an act of mercy. But one of the unfortunates was dragged forth from the ruins by the legs. They dragged him across the sand to the place best suited for the operation now in preparation. There the executioners held him fast, while others beautified his face and body with bayonet thrusts. A third group busied themselves gathering some smallish bits of wood for a small bonfire. Then the man was burned alive. More than one Englishman was present, more

than one officer was witness. None intervened. The
sepoy, half-consumed by the fire, now tried to free
himself from the torture. With a sudden exertion he
sprang out of the coals, drawing after him shreds and
tatters of stinking burnt flesh. After only a few steps he
was apprehended again. Again they laid him down on
his flaming bed, and this time they kept him there with
bayonet points until death nailed him fast. He is said to
have screamed unforgettably.

It's delightful to think that this is Kipling's India. It is
strange to reflect that it happened long after Keats had written
his odes to the nightingale, to a Grecian urn, and to autumn—
and it's likewise funny that Shelley had long since composed
his odes to the west wind and to intellectual beauty. Truth to
tell, Bernard Shaw was exactly one year old when the Sepoy
rebellion took place.

The *New York Daily Tribune* had at this time a young
Jewish London correspondent by the name of Karl Marx.
This young Marx was also active in the sphere of philosophy
and the political sciences. He gradually acquired something
of a name outside the columns of the *Daily Tribune.* But that's
another little story. And we shouldn't forget his activities as a
correspondent; he seems to have been an unusually alert and
well-informed journalist, who moreover possessed a certain
moral sense and great humanity. For such a young man he
had an extraordinarily wide horizon. One of his favorite subjects, remarkably enough, was colonial history. In 1857—in
other words, while George Bernard Shaw was still in
diapers—he writes, among other things, the following:

> The outrages committed by the revolted sepoys
> are indeed appalling, hideous, ineffable—such as one
> is prepared to meet only in wars of insurrection, of
> nationalities, of races and above all of religion; in one
> word, such as respectable England used to applaud
> when perpetrated by the Vendeans on the "Blues," by

the Spanish guerrillas on the infidel French, by
Serbians on their German and Hungarian neighbours,
by Croats on Viennese rebels, by Cavaignac's *Garde
mobile* on the sons and daughters of proletarian France.
However infamous the conduct of the sepoys, it is only
the reflex, in a concentrated form, of England's own
conduct in India, not only during the epoch of the
foundation of her Eastern Empire, but even during the
last ten years of a long-settled rule. To characterize that
rule, it suffices to say that torture formed an organic
institution of its financial policy.

This young man Marx had a truly original and independent mind. We shall dwell on him for a bit, not least because
for a journalist he shows an amazing wealth of knowledge. It's
also an appealing trait in a young man that he seems to have
a sort of allergy to atrocities. He goes on:

> For this purpose, we shall resort to the official Blue
> Books on the subject of East Indian torture, which
> were laid before the House of Commons during the
> sessions of 1856 and 1857. The evidence, it will be
> seen, is of a sort which cannot be gainsaid.
> We have first the report of the Torture
> Commission at Madras, which states its "belief in the
> general existence of torture for revenue purposes." It
> doubts whether "anything like an equal number of per-
> sons is annually subjected to violence on criminal
> charges, as for the fault of non-payment of revenue."

Likewise the Governor, Lord Dalhousie, writes in
September 1855 to the directors of the East India Company
that he has "long ceased to doubt that torture in one shape or
another is practised by the lower subordinates in every British
province."
Lord Dalhousie says further of a certain British District
Commissioner:

We have irrefragable proof that the officer has been guilty of each item in the heavy catalogue of irregularities and illegalities with which the Chief Commissioner has charged him, and which have brought disgrace on one portion of the British administration, and have subjected a large number of British subjects to gross injustice, to arbitrary imprisonment and cruel torture.

So much for the young Marx (one should take note of the name, since he will certainly make his mark in several fields). We should likewise remember the Governor's honesty. But people like Marx and Dalhousie have become rare in our time.

What's the purpose of it all?

Doesn't a cat have just as much ability to feel pain as an Indian, a black, or a human being?

I encountered the problem just the other day.

I found a large band of Arab boys in the street outside my lodgings, standing in a cluster. In the gutter in front of them lay—yes, exactly: a cat. I thought nothing of it, but walked on calmly across the Place des Martyrs, over to the little alcohol-free bar to get my coffee, black as pitch, and two big pastries of the Arab type. You have no idea what cakes are until you've lived in an Arab region. Arab writers have been singing the praises of these cakes for centuries. It sounds strange, but Islamic poets have always composed beautiful poems about cakes. While Villon sat in prison writing verses about how his corpse would look on the gallows, his Arab colleagues sat writing about cakes. I must confess that Islamic pastry deserves its poetic homage. The intense sweetness in the sugar glazes and in the mass of almonds inside the cake is kept in balance by the crispness and lightness of the pastry itself.

Of course there are also other things in Islamic cuisine which deserve their songs. I shall only mention a specialty like oven-baked sheep's head; the head is split lengthwise, and in each half you have one hemisphere of the brain. Strangely enough, they do the same thing in Iceland and the Faeroe Islands—but there they call it *smalhovud.* Otherwise the similarity invites something resembling a pun: Icelandic and Islamic—in both places you're served *smalhovud.* And the taste is the same, though the Arabs use more spices. The other day I ate *smalhovud* at an Arab restaurant; the trouble was that I had to go to a French restaurant to buy a bottle of wine to go with the sheep's head. Let no ill be said about the convolutions of a sheep's brain; they're very tasty.

After a breakfast of black coffee and Islamic cakes, I walked back to my own street. The boys were still standing there, but had moved to the other side of the road. They were throwing stones at something which lay where the cat had lain. But then I discovered that the cat was lying there still; it was just something about the color which was different. Pink and violet shone from it. Only when I came quite near did I see what it was: the cat's belly was ruptured, so that its intestines were exposed to the daylight. From breast to crotch the cat was split as if with a knife. Its whole belly had come open.

The boys were standing on the other side of the street and trying to hit the entrails, which were so clearly visible because of the beautiful colors—the cat was a common gray-striped one, rather dark. It lay still with its gaping belly upwards. It held its head half raised, and now and then shook it feebly. It didn't move its legs or its body. And actually it showed no sign of pain. The boys stopped throwing stones at its entrails when they saw that I didn't like it.

They explained to me that the cat had been run over by a truck, and that its belly had split when the wheel went over it. Then someone had nudged it into the gutter, and there it had remained. There was something almost obscene about the naked, exposed intestines. When I looked more closely, I saw that the cat had still found an expression for its pain. It would open its mouth halfway and hold it like that for a while, but without meowing; then it would slowly bare the teeth in its lower jaw, then close its mouth again. It was a wholly mute expression of pain, and only when you had noticed it did you receive the signal.

At first I didn't know what to do about the cat; but I couldn't let it lie there. Finally I laid the morning paper over it to cover up the obscene nakedness of the intestines. It answered by opening its mouth again and showing its lower teeth once more. Then I went back to the bar and asked them what I could do. They replied that there was a firm which ran animal ambulances, and I called it from the telephone booth.

Afterwards I stood for almost an hour and a half beside the cat, who showed no signs of dying or of fainting. It lay in exactly the same way, and I hoped that its spine had been broken so high up that it didn't feel the pain clearly. Finally a man came with a little van and donned thick leather gloves before he picked up the cat—but that wouldn't have been necessary, for it gave no sign of scratching or biting. On the other hand it meowed three or four times as it was being lifted into the car, and I had the feeling that it was addressing *me*. I paid the shamelessly high fee and stood there looking after the car for a while as it drove off to the clinic, where the cat would receive a gentle and loving injection and drift away on the wings of a merciful pharmacology.

When you come right down to it, doesn't this cat's death contain the whole history of bestiality? Isn't all our creaturely suffering already incorporated in this animal? My departed friend Johann Wolfgang the Great said: *Der Menschheit ganzer Jammer fasst mich an.* Yes, I'm grasped by the misery of all humanity.

The episode of the cat did not merely ruin the day for me; for several days, almost the whole week, I was conscious of the cat. It was a new reminder of the pain which is not my own.

When did I become like this?

What is the point of it all? What is the point of storing up inside me all the undeserved suffering which creation has gone through since the history of bestiality began—down to the injustice and the suffering which inheres in the present, and unfortunately in the future as well?

The darkness has closed around me once again. The rain mixing with dust in the street turns not to ordinary mud, but to a slimy bloody porridge, in which I wade and slide around. I know that if I fall down, I'll get all covered with this bloody muck, and I won't be able to get up again. I'll simply go on lying there, and drown in shit and blood.

I'd like to talk with Ali about this, but I don't know if it's right. Certain things one should keep to oneself. And yet Ali must know it indirectly—through the way I look at the world, and the way I ask questions.

It all has something to do with the revolution.

I simply want a rebellion against the whole world order. My revolution encompasses the universe. Something is wrong at the very bottom. There lies the root of evil.

Mea Culpa—Mea Maxima Culpa

What is it that has made me this way?

Childhood and death are the two things which play the greatest role for me. What lies between them is guilt. As children we are innocent, and when we're about to die we are innocent. As adults, in our active period, we manipulate things, we're busy doing things, wheeling and dealing and tilling our fields. We forget everything that counts; we forget that we're living on a planet which is slowly cooling and hardening. We forget the fire beneath us and the deadly cold above us. We forget that we *are*.

Only as children and only as we await death are we innocent. Only then do we remember that we came into this singular world knowing nothing about it, and will leave that same world without having understood a thing. Even generals, prime ministers, and corporation presidents become children again when they're about to die. Then they remember all that they had to forget in order to become what they became. They regain their innocence, and one can love them again. One can love them because they are once again filled with the great question.

Of all the world's miracles and wonders, none can compare with the fact that we have consciousness. Even the sea, the desert, the mountains, and the stars grow insignificant beside that consciousness which embraces everything. Within my own consciousness everything lies preserved. All my recollections, all the thousands and thousands of pictures—faces, cities, lands, seas.

Someone I met on the street in a big city, a young beggar and thief who lived on a staircase—he is within me. I no longer remember his name, but he was half-gypsy and dwells in my own interior, among all the pictures which fill me. I took him home to the hotel where I was staying, gave him food and money and let him wash his clothes in the bathroom. They dried on the radiator overnight. When he left the next day, he kissed me and presented me with a little lump of hashish and an old ballpoint pen as a memento. Those were all he owned.

Later in the day, as I sat drinking in the restaurant at the railway station, I saw him again; he didn't notice me. He was leaving now, going to a city where he had relatives. And he was wearing clean clothes—one of my shirts and his own newly-washed underwear. His socks were clean too.

He didn't smell.

It's good to go back home when one doesn't smell.

I've known statesmen and presidents of giant corporations, and none of them has gone out of his way to kiss me. Therefore I remember this hobo better.

In some way I must also have seen my own image in him. He came from nowhere, he didn't know who he was, and neither did he know where he was going or what was in store for him. Most assuredly we were brothers. He was poorer than I, but just as confused. And he fulfilled the commandment which is written: the Son of Man has no stone on which to lay his head.

There are thousands of pictures inside my consciousness; hundreds and hundreds of people. A deranged beggar in Southern Italy, a newly released convict in France.

How can my memory encompass so much? For gradually it all becomes part of myself. It becomes *me*. I have no other substance, no other existence, than these pictures I carry inside me.

How can I contain all this? How can I have become one with it?

I go down by the harbor, and again I see the hungry, vicious children. But now, in the daytime, I meet them singly, and they aren't dangerous. They kill only when it's dark and they are many.

Behind the big mole there are boats, big cabin cruisers and yachts. Here the revolution hasn't gone that far: some have pleasure boats and some move their bowels on the street. It's still like that, and it all has good reason to be the way it is. Communism doesn't mean eating porridge with a wooden ladle out of a common pot, as they say in Moscow. No indeed.

We often go out into the desert now, Ali and I. Out in one of the small oases something happened to me which nobody will believe. I met Alex on the street with his beloved—far inside Africa.

In the old days Alex used to introduce himself as "Alessandro, *il fundatore d'Alessandria.*" But it isn't quite true that he founded Alexandria. On the other hand, he's done a lot of other things. He was originally a record-keeper in the city of Berlin, but the Nuremburg laws drove him away. This highly intellectual, refined Berlin Jew went to France and became a soldier. In Africa he fought in the French Foreign Legion against his Teutonic countrymen.

The rest of the story is so wildly improbable that I'm ashamed to tell it. Only astrologists will believe it.

He was living in Berlin with his beloved when Adolf came. Both of them had to get out. She fled by way of Holland to America. From there, for some crazy reason, she went to China, to Shanghai.

Alex fought in France and then in Africa; every battle which could be lost to the Teutons, he helped to lose. Finally he ended up as a refugee in China.

In Shanghai they met on the street.

I too met them on the street—in a little South Italian fishing town. They were on the trail of an old friend and fellow record-keeper of Alessandro's. He was named Loevi and had also been driven from Teutonia by Adolf's racist laws. Earlier he had written most of his newspaper articles under the pseudonym "al Assadun." He disappeared from the Third Reich and settled in an unknown South Italian fishing village, where he went safely underground.

There he had mysteriously vanished, nor had he ever been seen again in his old home town of Berlin. Loevi had simply disappeared. But the two Alessandros hadn't given up hope of finding their old friend again.

Now they were combing the Italian fishing villages—not such an unpleasant task in itself, when you think how cozy these little towns are, and what good cuisine they have.

But the town where we met had never housed any German refugee. At least none of the natives could remember one, and in such a small place they couldn't possibly have forgotten him if he had stayed there.

Alex and his beloved and I often ate together, and with great culinary profit, at one of the little fish *trattorias;* we drank our white wine and enjoyed our fish soup there. We talked about the utter meaninglessness of life and the certain advent of the revolution. Often, too, we talked with the proprietor or with the guests.

Now you mustn't think that our fishing town was a completely godforsaken corner of the world. Both one thing and another had happened there, and through the years it had been visited by many traveling folk. The one who had made the greatest impression on people was a wandering Arab who had settled in the village and had gone on living there until his death. He had been a friendly soul and a deeply religious person who, unrolling the prayer rug which he almost always carried with him, faithfully performed his prayers three times a day. And the town showed him all the kindness and friendliness which is typical for Italians of limited means. He became very popular, and when he died it turned out that he was also genuinely loved.

This town lies as if hewn into the mountain wall, and its cemetery is situated rather high up, several hundred feet above the town itself. The graveyard is like a small shelf cut into the steep wall of rock; and all the earth which they needed to bury the dead, they had had to carry in baskets and pails up the hundreds of stairs on the narrow winding path which led there.

Now when the man died, the town elders gathered to decide what they should do with their dead Saracen. They resolved to bury him at public expense, since he had left neither property nor kin, but only the memory of a devout and homeless heathen. And they acknowledged his religious turn of mind by erecting a real monument over him—a stela nearly as tall as a man, shaped like a colossal penis. On the stone they carved the Musselman's name.

It is no exaggeration to say that he was a beloved and esteemed citizen of the town when he passed away.

One evening the two Alessandros and I went up to the cemetery to enjoy the incredible view of the sea and the setting sun. Below us lay the ocean, dark blue and so massive that it seemed to be cast in cement. And as we stood up there on that ledge where the cemetery lay, we saw for the first time how precipitous the mountainside was. You could get vertigo from less than that. We also eagerly studied the mighty stone phallus which the town had erected in honor of the Arab's memory.

His name was chiseled in both Italian and Arabic. His Italianized name read: "Leone."

"Funny that he was called 'Leone'," said Alex; "that means 'lion'."

"It's a rather common name here," I replied; "in Swedish it's called *lejon*—there too they've adopted the Latin form."

This was at a time when I was trying to teach myself Arabic—an undertaking which failed miserably, owing to the student's weak willpower and lax character.

"What does it say in Arabic?" asked Alessandro's beloved.

"It says . . ." I replied; "wait a minute, it says. . . ."

Slowly and carefully I began spelling my way through the Arabic consonants. Finally they became a word.

"What does it say?" Alex asked.

"It says 'al-Assadun'," I replied, "or 'al-Assadon'—the Arabs aren't very particular about vowels. It means 'lion'."

"al Assadun?" he said: "al Assadun . . . that reminds me of something. . . . Now what is it?"

They looked at each other. Both appeared unwilling to believe their eyes.

"Leone, al Assadun, Loevi," she said.

"So here you lie," Alex went on. "Whoever would have dreamed that you would be buried with your face toward Mecca?"

"And that the cynical old pig would become famous for his religious turn of mind!" she said.

"Here he was considered a model for the religious education of the young," I added; "even the priest showed deep respect for the infidel."

Not very long before this, oddly enough, an American magazine had run a lengthy article about the Saracen who, settling among Italian fishermen, had gradually become like one of the natives, except that he clung to his religion. The magazine was aimed primarily at tourists and other travelers, and it therefore took an interest in strange stories from distant lands and realms. Of course the author had no idea that the immigrant was a literary Jew from Berlin.

Thus—in connection with Loevi-Assadun—I got to know the two Alessandros. I also learned something from them—about China.

"Which of the occupations was the worst?" I asked Alex over the fish soup. He chewed a couple of mussels and swallowed them.

"The American," he replied promptly. "They had a habit, when they got drunk, of throwing the Chinese in the water. And the Chinese, as everybody knows, can't swim. They couldn't swim in the old days; they've never been able to swim. And so when the Americans were looking for some fun, they'd take one and throw him into the water, and there he'd stay, thrashing about, until he drowned. It was their chief

amusement. This thing about the Chinese not being able to
swim has become a national inferiority complex, and that's
the background for Mao's swims in the Yellow River. The
country is learning to swim to show that they're like other
people. Nobody seems to have discovered the political and
didactic background of these swims."

"How was it when the Communists took over?" I said.

"It was as if Heaven had come down to earth," he replied.

"Suddenly there were no more children lying dead on the
streets," she said. "That's the standard one must apply to the
revolution: the children, dead of starvation, who were always
lying in your way when you wanted to go out."

Neither of them was a believing Communist.

"Only in China has the revolution achieved what a revolution must if it is to be successful: namely, a fast and visible
bettering of conditions. If you can't substantially improve living conditions for the majority, the revolution has failed and
you'll have to maintain it by force and violence, guns and
secret police, soldiers and tanks."

"In short, Eastern Europe?"

"Yes—Eastern Europe."

We often discuss revolutions, but never the last war or fas-
cism any more. We've talked enough about that.

There seems to be a peculiar and unvarying dynamic
built into nearly all revolutions; they begin as liberation
movements, with insurrections and guerrilla wars; after
they've defeated the former rulers, and the improvements
fail to materialize and all the aims of the revolution are lost
from view, they change into fascistoid dictatorships in which
power merely serves to maintain power. The symptoms of
the process are many and well-known, and they recur again
and again.

Yes, the Alessandros and I had many conversations, and
we ate many meals together.

Afterwards it went as it so often does with friendships: for
awhile we wrote to each other, then the letters gradually
stopped coming, and you thought of the others once in

awhile—then you lost the address, and finally the whole thing was only a half-forgotten memory.

Several years after we'd been together in our little town where the bogus Arab had lived and died, we met on the street in Berlin.

We picked up our conversation as if we'd seen each other the day before. We got to know each other all over again. All of us had changed to some extent, and it was again exciting to talk.

Then followed the same process once more. We wrote letters, and gradually the letters became penny postcards. Then the penny postcards became picture postcards, and so the correspondence ebbed out. A few stray thoughts remained. Then the address got lost again, and gradually everything once more became a memory. Several years passed.

Then I met both Alessandros again on the street in a dusty, godforsaken little oasis far inside the Sahara. For a while we just stood looking at each other; none of us would stoop to believing that this was real. But there it was: I was I—and the Alessandros were the Alessandros. It was quite simply true.

I introduced them to Ali, and it turned out that we'd all been on the way to one and the same decaying hotel to eat. If we hadn't met on the street, we would have ended up in the dining room, sitting at adjoining tables. There we couldn't have avoided recognizing each other.

Now that I think about it, our chance meeting in the really big city of Berlin was arranged in the same idiotic manner; both parties were on the way to the same theater and the same performance—the two Alessandros even had tickets for the seats behind me. We couldn't have avoided meeting there either.

The only one who didn't find the encounter the least bit strange was Ali; there was nothing odd about it to an African, he said in German:

"We are used to wizards and the supernatural; no true African sees anything striking or peculiar in such meetings."

"How do you explain it?" I asked.

"Hm," said Ali: "It's something in the direction of what Jung calls the collective unconscious, but I also think that it has to do with an individual unconscious, something which is more or less strongly developed."

"In other words, an unconscious self which guides and directs us?" I said.

Alex was listening attentively.

"Yes," said Ali. "A self we don't know, but which is stronger and more determinative than the aware and conscious self that we're familiar with."

"Can these two selves establish contact with each other?"

"Of course; that's what we call wizardry—or magic, if you will. To you Europeans, of course, it's all black superstition and lunacy. To us the supernatural is just as natural as plants and trees, animals and human beings. Our everyday experience of this unconscious inner self is our conscience and our sense of right."

"The starry sky above me and the moral law within me," said Alex, smiling warmly.

"Is that the metaphysics of the revolution?" I said.

"It's all the same to me whether you call it metaphysics or magic," replied Ali.

"And what happens to this unconscious, unknown self when the body dies?"

"It waits until it finds a new body to take up residence in, of course."

"And this you reconcile with Marx?" I asked.

"Yes, of course," he replied; "with the greatest of ease."

"So what does Marx say about it?"

"He maintains complete silence. This thing about spirits or the unconscious self, it's the religion of my fathers, and it's not one whit more absurd or barbarian than Christianity's trinity and virgin birth. By the way, if you want a more European word for the spirits of the dead, you can use Goethe's designation for the immortal in man: *entelechy*. Does that sound better?"

"Yes," I replied, "that sounds undeniably more civilized. One can almost accept it. Can't you tell us more from the jungle?"

"No," said Ali, "I'd rather hear what the two Alessandros have to tell from Asia. I've never been there, and I have an immediate question: The Christians completely destroyed all the original American and African cultures, but in India their destructive efforts only came close to succeeding, in China they didn't come so close—and in Japan they didn't manage to destroy much of anything. The Europeanizing of Japan took place only to the degree that the Japanese themselves wanted it, in the form of technological development and industry. Why didn't the whites manage to destroy Asia totally?"

We seated ourselves at a dusty table in the abandoned dining room of the hotel—which, incidentally, bore the name "Hôtel de Boulogne." We ordered peppers stuffed with mutton, and wine, cheese, and fruit. The heat was now intense, and I sat there bathed in sweat. The air stood still and quivered with the heat. The drops ran from my forehead and scalp down into my eyes, over my nose, along my cheeks, over my lips and mouth, and collected under my chin or ran on down my neck and chest. In a moment I was sticky wet. None of the others was sweating the way I was, though the fiercely seasoned hors d'œuvres forced out drops on their faces as well. Alex waited a bit before answering Ali's question. Then he said:

"There are a number of different reasons for that. Two of them—one applies to India and China, the other to Japan—are quite enlightening and easily understood.

"First you have China's and India's enormous age and population; the Asian cultures are the oldest. They're sure of themselves. Asia and parts of Africa are thus actually the first world, the Americas the second—and Europe, the United States, and Russia are the third world. In other words, precisely the reverse of how the Europeans themselves see it.

"Their age alone gives the Indian and Chinese cultures an enormous strength and stability—and their highly developed

religions and philosophies give them a powerful self-aware-
ness, so that they feel Christianity and the white man's unruly
trading instinct and greed as primitive and immature. On top
of this, of course, there's also the immobility of inertia, stemming from the sheer size of the population. Neither the
Chinese nor the Indians have let themselves be Christianized;
they would feel the conversion to Christianity as a regression,
a reduction of their human dignity.

"In Japan the situation is different. Japan has chosen strict
isolation on her islands. The Japanese themselves are an
imperialistic and warlike people, in contrast to the Chinese,
who are deeply peace-loving—and the Japanese saw through
the whites. Being cut of the same cloth, they knew how dangerous the European influence could become. All the way up
to the atom bombs over Nagasaki and Hiroshima they knew
it, and they know it still.

"The interesting thing, though, is that the Japanese saw
through the Christian missionaries and their Christianity.
They also understood, better than any of the others, the monstrous cheek, the indescribable gall, of the whites' desire to
proselytize there. They were deeply offended by the hubris of
the whites—in this case especially the shamelessly greedy
Portuguese bloodsuckers—by the arrogance of the exploiters
in coming to a foreign country with a high, autonomous culture and saying: Our religion is better than yours! We have
the right god, and now you must learn that God has revealed
the truth only to us!

"It's astonishing how few Christians comprehend what
indescribable spiritual arrogance lies in the whole idea of
missionizing.

"And the Japanese refused to be exploited, but their first
target wasn't the soldiers or the shopkeepers from Europe.
They saw more deeply into the matter: they understood that
the main problem was the whites' missionary zeal and their
narcissistic religion. They understood that the real threat to
Japan's autonomy lay in *Christianity*, which was deeply foreign and inimical to their people's distinctive nature.

"By the end of the sixteenth century Christianity had
already been outlawed in Japan. But when the priests and the
missionaries, in defiance of the country's laws and government, continued to foist their Christianity and their hope of
heaven on the defenseless poor, the ban gradually developed
into a persecution of the Christians. The Christians were maltreated, tortured, and sometimes executed in rather ingenious
ways. That was Japan's answer.

"At this time the Christian Church, for obvious reasons,
was in need of new martyrs; and the Church sent young and
fanatical priests illegally to Japan. These were then apprehended, and were duly made into martyrs. The Church was
soon deeply indebted to the Japanese executioners.

"The main thing, however, was that Christianity was erad-
icated. But that wasn't enough; matters came to such a pass
that Japan also broke off trade relations with the zealous
Portuguese. That hurt.

"For these reasons—Japan's isolation and her well-
founded mistrust of the whites—the Europeans never managed to destroy the country's culture, economy, or political
independence. Japan never became a European colony."

Ali heaved a heavy, painful sigh:

"It must have been hard on the Portuguese not to be
allowed to do the same in Japan as in Africa or America.
They were allowed neither to burn the natives alive, nor to
baptize them, nor to sack the country. The Japanese thought
that Japan belonged to the inhabitants and not to the Church.
And throughout Christendom there arose a great wailing over
the Japanese atrocities—at a time when the Church was wal-
lowing in heretic and witch trials—wiping out whole provinces, torturing and burning."

"The Japanese torturers," Alex went on, "were sometimes
quite inventive, but they were novices in the art compared to
the Church's chirurgical experts."

I sat there in silence, listening. Together they gorged on
hatred of Europe. Ali and the two Alessandros had found
each other—far inside the Sahara, in a threadbare oasis.

There's something special about Europe, something I long
for:

It came to pass in those days that God had allowed the
Devil to leave Hell and seek a cooler lodging among the children of men. According to that great *cognoscente* of men and
devils, Niccolo Machiavelli, the Black Majesty and fallen
angel had atoned for his rebelliousness long enough. As a residence on earth among his two-legged brethren the Devil
quite naturally chose Tuscany's capital—city of flowers, city
of blood—Fiorenzia, the city of trade and anthems.

This happened at the beginning of the 1400's, *quattrocento.*
At first the Devil felt right at home in Florence; he lied and
cheated like all the rest, and soon became a true Florentine.

From Hell (which is Pluto's realm) he had brought with
him a fortune of seven million gold florins—a great deal of
money in those days—which he now proposed to multiply by
putting them to work with, among others, the city's bankers
and merchants. Had there been insurance companies back
then, he would naturally have invested in them. In their
absence, the Devil chose the expedient of investing parts of
his fortune with the city's most honest and upright usurers.

Next he bought a *castello* which had belonged to a bankrupt noble family, and a count's title to go with it; whereupon
he married the youngest daughter of a prominent but finan-
cially shaky politician. The Devil gave a thousand florins to
the city's poor and five hundred thousand to the Church,
after which he calmly looked forward to a tranquil old age.

Now, of course, you'd think that all was well and good,
but unfortunately it's right here that the story of the Devil and
the Florentines begins. The poor fellow was an easy mark for
them—so naive and generous he had grown after serving his
eleven thousand years in hell and thereby settling his
accounts with his God.

His wondrously beautiful, fourteen-year-old wife—the age

difference was a problem in itself—inaugurated their union by buying five new palaces. Then she refused to perform her marital duties until he had bought her a coach of, so to speak, pure gold. Her jewel collection won renown all over Tuscany, and the countess's father rose in social worth from mere prominence to a position of real influence. He also provided his less affluent colleagues with cash loans from his patient son-in-law's bank account.

The young wife's needs mounted daily; her staff of servants multiplied into a nation, and on top of that she took young, handsome lovers from poor families—persons who also merited the quondam majesty's economic support. Even worse, however, was the idiom which the Countess gradually came to use toward her spouse. She had learned the art of moral flagellation. He was insulted and mocked; in the presence of guests and servants he was humiliated time and time again. And when that wasn't enough, she didn't shrink from corporal chastisement. He often had his ears boxed or his hair pulled. And his life's companion had a tongue which was not merely virulent and murderous, but unstoppable as well. Even when the Devil was sitting on the privy, she would stand outside and harangue him. Her tongue didn't rest all day, and when night came and the lamps were extinguished, when the peace of slumber should have settled over him, she went on scolding in her sleep.

Meanwhile he also had a mother-in-law of ancient Florentine lineage, and the daughter was but a pale shadow of her mother. If the young Countess was hungry as a wolf after her spouse's gold ducats, the old one pursued her son-in-law's like a tigress. Her craving for new palaces, brocades, jewels, and servants was insatiable. The Devil put up with it all out of dread and a desire to keep the peace. It was worst when both mother and daughter jumped on him at once; they screamed, they hissed, they accused him of hiding his money, of pettiness, and of disgracing his wife's family with his boundless greed.

The Devil had long suffered from painful nocturnal sweats, nightmares, and attacks of dread and palpitations. On top of this he had trouble breathing as well. After four years of marriage he likewise became prey to frequent and violent crying jags. Besides, the Devil drank much more than was good for him.

Out of terror he paid everything the ladies demanded, consoling himself with the thought that most of his gold florins were in safe hands with his friends the bankers, the merchants, and the money lenders, all of whom would increase his millions by using them for the exploitation of Tuscany's poor. The bankers were seizing bankrupt estates, the merchants were huckstering, and the usurers were practicing usury. Society was functioning as it should.

Or so he thought.

In other words: the Devil thought that he was on the side of the grave-robbers, not one of their victims.

But then a remarkable thing happened: His capital reaped no dividends. The blood and tears of the poor notwithstanding, his gold florins dried up. Every time a moneylender, a merchant, or a banker did some good business, there were unimpeachable accounts to show that the Devil's ducats had no part in the returns. Quite the contrary.

After five years the seven million had shrunk to one and a half.

The women screamed, his father-in-law cursed, and the businessmen feared for their profits. They all suspected him of embezzling his own funds and maybe keeping something for himself. It was rumored that he was insolvent.

The scenes with his wife and mother-in-law mounted from the terrifying to the intolerable.

A year later the flight from his creditors began. They were determined to flay him alive. They woke him at night, sent dunning and threatening letters daily, harassed him in public, demanded forced auction and the debtor's prison.

Now he *was* insolvent.

Which he feared most, the women or the creditors, nobody knows. But half-crazed with terror he certainly was— a quaking, tear-soaked bundle of nerves.

Whether the Florentines had bedeviled or out-deviled him is hard for a layman to say. During an autumn storm, in the dark and gloom of night, he swung himself onto his horse and disappeared.

The next morning his wife and mother-in-law met with the creditors. They were agreed that he had swindled them all, and together they took up the chase.

Masked and exhausted, the Devil arrived in the town of Peretola in Tuscany, where he put up at an inn. All he had with him besides his horse were his everyday clothes and a little leather purse of gold ducats. That was all he owned.

The first thing he did was to fling himself on the bed in his room, where he broke into paroxysms of weeping. He knew that his women and his creditors were now beating the bushes for him all over Tuscany, and he shook with terror.

During his stay in Peretola he often strolled around the city, always in disguise and always prepared for a new flight. On one of his walks he was witness to a public execution which had drawn a good crowd. First the delinquent was subjected to long and thorough pinching with red-hot tongs; then they broke all his bones, and in this broken condition he was threaded onto the wheel, which was then mounted on a stake. Finally, to the crowd's great delight, they cut his tongue out of his mouth.

Such death scenes—mostly staged by the Church, and sometimes much more refined and well-plotted—the Devil had often witnessed in Florence; and as he stood observing the execution here in Peretola, he was seized with the melancholy thought that this was his only real profit from his sojourn on the earth's surface: he had learned a great many new and choice methods of torture—which showed once again how far Hell had fallen behind.

The same afternoon, while the Devil was in his room, he heard horses' hooves and the squeaking of wheels from the street. Hiding behind the mullioned window he peered down anxiously, and at once his anxiety changed to panic; the procession which was advancing into the city consisted of his wife, his mother-in-law, three of his worst and most ruthless creditors, and four bailiffs from Florence. Now the Devil knew that it was only a question of hours before the ladies would get their claws into him, and he decided to try the very last resort. Still sweaty and trembling, he locked and bolted his door; then with a piece of chalk he drew a five-pointed star on the floor and knelt in the center of it.

"Dear God!" prayed the Prince of Darkness; "Dear God, hear me!"

"What is it, my son?" answered the Lord.

"Help me away from here! Save me from the Florentines!" said the Devil.

"What's wrong with the Florentines?" asked God.

"You must know that; you created them!"

"Say what it is!"

"They're known over half the world for their poisonous tongues, their devilish laughter, and their villainy in money matters," replied the Devil.

"Perhaps you'd rather go to Spain?"

"No, no! Anywhere but there! We have enough inquisition here!"

"What do you want, then?" asked God kindly.

"I want to go home. I want to go back to Hell," said the Devil.

"My son, your wish shall be granted. I feared something of the sort."

"Thanks, Lord," replied the Devil: "Thy will be done!"

And with a crash the Evil One vanished through the floor—the shortest route from Peretola to Hell; where, according to the greatest theologians, he resides to this very day.

This melancholy truth about the Devil's furlough from Hell has something to do with the town of Peretola, and may explain what happened there not long afterwards.

For precisely in this selfsame Peretola it pleased God to let the house of Vespucci live and prosper. The family distinguished itself in many ways; in 1490, for example, the eleven-year-old Giovanni Vespucci translated Sallust's *Catalina* from

Latin into the tongue of his fathers, Tuscan.

In this family lived a man by the name of Nastacio Vespucci, and Nastacio begat Amerigo, whose name was to be immortalized, and who first saw the darkness of this world in the year 1451—the same year that Cristofo Colombo was born.

One found the way to the New World, and the other received the credit; it was later baptized in his name—America. But there was no hatred or enmity between the two men.

This singular deviation from the normal—their being good friends—was due to two things: In the first place neither of them was a proper criminal, man of violence, torturer, and murderer like the Conquistadors and their henchmen, the priests; both possessed a dash of pure scientific interest in *il Mondo Nuovo*. Of course they also had an eye to the ducats, but who doesn't? In the second place, they in fact divided the continent between them; each explored his own part. Amerigo Vespucci was the first European to set his not exactly newly-washed foot in Brazil. Like the bandits who came after him, he believed that he had come to the earthly Paradise, to the world before the Fall—a land which God had never destroyed, but merely moved from the Tigris and Euphrates. It was a land where the people knew nothing of sin and guilt, and lived together in love.

That he received the credit for finding the continent was due, strangely enough, to a misunderstanding by a certain printer in Lorraine, or Lothringen—who, while printing a book which was to be a bestseller, had the misfortune to per-petuate his ignorance by making Amerigo the discoverer of the whole continent; but that's another story.

Vespucci based his Paradise theory not only on the beauty and hospitality of both the nature and the people, but also on the fact that in Brazil there reigned absolute promiscuity with-out the slightest feeling of guilt: father lay with daughter, sis-ter with sister, brother with brother, mother with son, they all lived in the deepest innocence. Later on, handier folk came to the country, and they were well-versed in the art of trans-forming a paradise into a hell. It's strange that the good padre

Las Casas, who took the *indios'* part against the whites, should himself become the cause of such great misery. He saw that the Indians were dying from forced labor under the whips of their white masters; and to spare the natives who couldn't endure the work, he proposed importing slaves from Africa. This provided the impetus for the rise of the slave trade. Here we see a most instructive example of how our best thoughts of God can be turned to evil and bear poisonous fruit.

But concerning Amerigo himself, I must think of what Columbus said to me once down by the harbor next to the mosque:

"Amerigo was the first to understand that the world we had come to wasn't China or India, but a new, separate continent; and therefore it was right that it should receive his name."

I hadn't met Columbus for a long time. When I met him again just now, he was in many ways a changed man. He had grown older and more stoop-shouldered. And there was a dullness, a sallowness about him. His sun-bleached seaman's eyes had gotten lighter, and his hair was almost white. The dark and light spots in his face and on his hands—which old sailors get when they've sailed a great deal in tropical waters—were even more noticeable than before. His clothes were faded and seemed very worn, as well as terribly out of date. And on top of that he was shaking violently, and not only in his hands; it was mostly his head and face which quivered.

"Fancy seeing you again!" said Columbus: "You look exhausted; are you still working on the history of bestiality?"

"Yes," I said, "but the end is in sight. I'm more interested in revolutions now."

"Have you grown reconciled with the world?" he went on, taking my arm in his characteristic, friendly manner.

"No," I said.

"Won't you ever give up?"

"No," I replied, "never."

"Well, well," he said; "the world is full of injustice."

The hungry children thronged around us, and to get away

from them we went into one of the little fish restaurants. Of course one never escapes from the Arab children, they'll stand outside and wait until you leave the place—but at least one can get a moment's peace.

We ordered fish soup and fried shrimp—followed by salad, peaches, and Arabian coffee with brandy on the side.

"The children," said Columbus, his face quivering; "it was just like that in my time too. Always the hungry youngsters. Always the poor children—in Portugal, in Spain, and in my fatherland, Italy. But on the Caribbean islands—among the Indians—it wasn't like that. When we arrived, there weren't any hungry children there."

"Today there are lots of them," I said: "There are millions of hungry children in Latin America. Masses. . . ."

"So sad," said Columbus. His face quivered. At the same time he shook his head.

"It's most deplorable," he went on; "all the hungry children."

"Yes, yes," I said.

He was silent for a moment, as if talking to himself; then he added:

"It happened with my help. I'm not blameless in this."

He raised his right hand and crossed himself.

"*Mea culpa*," he mumbled; "*mea maxima culpa.*"

For awhile we ate in silence. And we drank wine and broke bread between us.

"Columbus," I said, "I have a question about something else."

He looked up:

"Yes?"

"Is it true that the *Santa Maria* measured only seventy-eight feet?"

He looked at me pensively, thinking it over carefully.

"No," he replied slowly, "she was seventy-eight feet and six inches."

"And on her you sailed to the Caribbean islands. What would have happened if you had hit a cyclone?"

He smiled—a pale, indulgent smile:

"That would have been a good thing for the Indians."

"Oh?"

"We would have been blown to shreds at the first gust."

He sat still for awhile, shook his head, and smiled again. I saw that he had pictures inside him, and that he was mulling them over. Then he repeated:

"At the first gust!"

It was obvious that in some way he was enjoying the thought.

"What makes people risk their lives in such a crazy fashion?" I said.

"Ambition and greed," he replied.

"How's that?"

"Fame and gold."

"Is that all?" I said.

"Yes," he replied, "that's all."

Then something strange happened before my very eyes: his outline blurred, and he seemed to be growing smaller.

"There must be something more," I said.

He shook his head, and I saw that his lips were moving; he was clearly straining to say something. I bent forward, and he whispered very faintly:

"Yes, there was also something else. . . ."

Now it was clear that he was getting smaller. He was also growing steadily less visible; little by little he became transparent. At the same time he shriveled up. He shrank and shrank, growing steadily more diaphanous. Presently he was tiny and almost invisible. Then he was gone.

Because I dreaded meeting the children outside after the meal, I lingered over another bottle of wine. And I fixed my thoughts upon the solar system and the root of evil, and where the basis for the misery lies. In and of itself the solar system functions splendidly; one mustn't expect too much from it. The sun sings its ancient, mighty song for the just and the unjust, and it's surrounded by lovely lifeless planets where no wrong ever happens. It's only our own globe, young Gaea, which presents difficulties—in other words, the earth is the solar system's only problem planet. It follows that the reason, the Root of Evil, must be sought here. But I love this planet!

Through the window I could see the western sky growing red; soon the sun would conclude its golden journey. Soon it would be dark outside. Like swift shadows I glimpsed the children out there; their hour was approaching.

Of course it sounds absurd and idiotic in the extreme to say that we are accomplices in the misery. My own culpability in what has happened, and is happening still, does not lie on the plane of action; strictly speaking I've never hurt a fly, never done an evil act of any magnitude; I've never killed, never tortured anyone. Any idiot of an American sergeant is a greater sinner than I. If I myself am more guilty, then the guilt, the complicity, lies in another sphere: in my way of thinking. It's not my deeds, it's my thoughts which are culpable. Here we approach the Root of Evil.

So long as one thinks European, one is an accomplice in the crimes. Until one has learned to think un-European, one stands in the service of evil. At first it can be hard enough to stop thinking nationalistically—then, if one manages that, one goes over into thinking in the concepts and prejudices and misconceptions of the continent, of the race. Then it's a matter of seeing Europe and the whole white culture from outside. Finally one must see the planet from outside—all cultures must be regarded from the perspective of distance, with suspicion's well-honed look. We've seen the Milky Way from the earth long enough; now it's time to see the earth from the Milky Way. When you come right down to it, Gaea—in her character as the only problem planet—is the center of the solar system. Our cosmography has once again become geocentric.

The question is: What is the matter with this planet, what is it that went wrong after such a splendid beginning?

The first thing that's wrong, of course, is that on Gaea there is life; no one has ever been oppressed or maltreated on the moon. And which is better: planets in lifeless, eternal innocence, or our living, blood-reeking globe?

The Root of Evil lies deep in our flesh; it stretches a long way back. Ever since life began, life has lived by preying. Ever since the earliest known formation of larger societies, people have oppressed, exploited, and enslaved each other. The injustice has been continuous.

What matters is to determine what guises it's taking today. We've seen theocracies and monarchies and aristocracies, and we've seen the rule of the bourgeoisie, of the shopkeepers. All have built on pure violence and the oppression of the weak. We've seen juntas, bureaucracies, and technocracies.

But we've also seen revolutions; we know that somewhere there are limits to injustice. We've seen revolutions fail, and we've seen that things can improve. We've also seen them lead to more injustice.

The revolution which is needed must be a total upheaval, from the very bottom; but before we can achieve it, we must know what a human being is. And we don't know that at present.

Must we adapt society to the individual, or the individual to society?

We're talking of vast dimensions now. Only the stars and the sea can compare with the Revolution. That's how the Revolution must be this time.

I bought a couple of extra portions of bread so as to have something to dole out to the children when I had to leave. Not out of compassion—these crumbs don't help anybody— but for purely practical reasons: to get by them in peace. I have the impression that they're even more aggressive now than they were before.

I walked up toward the main streets. Darkness settled over the great African city as the lamps were being lit. In these first evening hours there are masses of people on the streets, people in African or European clothes. And I noticed the aroma of food from the restaurants and of black coffee from the bars, everywhere the odors filtered out, mixed with light and voices. Here and there they were playing Arab music.

Ali was shot at on the street a few days ago. Now we know that the police spies from his homeland have found him. That means he'll have to change his name and place of residence once again.

I long for Europe.

Slowly I walked up the broad boulevard; between the cafés and the restaurants stood the rows of expensive luxury shops. Now and then I stopped in front of a window to look at the merchandise. There were goods of every conceivable origin—English men's clothes and leather goods, elegant shoes and gloves; there were French perfumes, women's clothes from the biggest fashion houses in Europe, but also things from India, and fishing and hunting tackle from America. Most often I stopped before windows displaying native clothes and jewelry, or goods from the neighboring African countries. The long and rather close-fitting dresses— or caftans—were made of pure, heavy silk and reached from the chin to the ankles. Often they were covered with embroidery, ornamented in various colors along the collar and facings—always with taste and beauty, never overloaded. There were garments costing several thousand francs apiece. I stopped to stare at a caftan which had massive gold embroidery from the neck to the feet. Someone pulled at my coatsleeve.

I turned my head and looked around. Beside me stood a very dark girl of twelve or thirteen; she stretched out a thin brown hand and said:

"Monsieur?"

I recognized her at once from the harbor. She belonged to the flock of children which begged there, and was somewhat bigger than most of them. She had nothing on under her thin dress. She was faintly negroid.

"Monsieur?" she repeated, stretching her hand further in my direction.

"No," I said: "Go away!"

I knew that if I gave her anything now, she'd never leave me in peace again. She was still holding onto my sleeve.

I tore myself loose and walked on. She didn't give up, she sprang past me and turned, then danced backwards in front of me up the street, shrieking loudly and piercingly:

"Monsieur! Monsieur! Give me something! Just a little, monsieur!"

It was painful, because her shrieks were so loud that they attracted attention. People turned to look at us. I kept walking, with the dancing devil-child in front of me. She knew that it was annoying, and persisted with even wilder movements and even louder shrieks:

"Only a few pennies, monsieur! Monsieur!"

More and more people turned to look. What she wanted was quite clear; I should be pressed into parting with a few centimes. But I didn't give in; pretending that nothing was amiss, I went on as if I neither saw nor heard her. We came to a corner a little way off the main street with its lighted shops, and all at once she leapt forward and grabbed my arm. She pulled me around the corner and into the shadows.

It was dusky there, and from the boulevard it would look entirely dark. The moment we were in the shadows she lifted her dress all the way up to her navel and stood there naked from the waist down. Her black eyes glittered.

"Monsieur," she said, "shall I come home with you?"

I didn't answer. I looked at her thin underparts and at the curly hair framing her brown face. She smiled, then put one hand to her crotch and rubbed herself there a couple of times.

"Monsieur," she said, "I only want five francs."

She took my hand, still holding up her dress:

"Only five francs," she repeated.

"Listen," I said: "You're little. I'm a grown man."

"I'm not little!"

"Yes, you are," I said. "It's impossible."

She was silent for a moment, then she said:

"Monsieur can come into me from behind if monsieur wants."

She turned and presented her naked rump to me, then with her fingers she parted her seat muscles and showed me her small, pale-brown rectum.

"There," she said: "It's easier that way, monsieur."

That would have given her a nice hold on me next time I met her in the flock!

"Listen!" I said: "Turn around!"

She let go of her dress and turned to face me. Her shining eyes were black as coal.

"Yes, monsieur?"

"I'll give you five francs right here," I said, "If you promise to leave me in peace and not run after me."

I held out my hand with the money. She took the note, and at once her thin fingers closed around it.

"Shan't I come home with monsieur?" she said: "Since he's paid me the five francs?"

"No," I replied; "maybe another time."

"Monsieur knows where I am. I'm always down by the docks. I sleep there."

She looked up at me, a long and solemn look. She seemed disappointed; then she started walking. She walked slowly, with her hand clenched firmly around the note. And a thought struck me.

It's strange how we recoil at the thought of pleasuring ourselves with minors, it's as if the world would go under if we did. And it's forbidden; had I so much as touched her with my hand while she was showing me her small charms, I would have qualified myself for several years in prison.

On the other hand, it is lawful to kill children. That's less harmful. In some cases there's an outright bounty on the little darlings. One can exterminate them with dynamite, with phosphorus, or with napalm and fragmentation bombs—and the child-murderers from the Wehrmacht, the RAF, and the American Air Force receive shiny medals with eagles and lions to wear on their patriotic breasts just for knocking off a few hundred of them.

But if they touched the neighbor's little daughter under

her dress, they'd be put in the pen for a long, long time. And be disgraced for life besides.

I looked after her as she wandered down the street in the light from the shop windows.

She was walking quietly, but now and then she'd make a little hop with her left leg, and come down again on the same foot. Then she'd amble on, still with one hand clenched. No one should see her treasure.

I know why she had looked disappointed for a moment: she had hoped for a place to sleep.

The darkness has sunk all the way over me now. I lie in bed and hear that he has come into my room—he who has followed me, waited for me, ever since I was a child. Finally, down here south of Mare Nostrum, he has caught up with me. I can hear him breathing in the darkness, over by the door. I lie here like a bundle of dread and alcohol. He's breathing very softly, slowly, but toward the end of each inhalation his breathing rises to a faint snort, as if he were nervous or anxious now—now that he's about to act, to accomplish his mission. I know he's in here. I feel the cold from him. Never have I felt him so near before.

The darkness comes like a blow. It can fall on me in mid-thought, in mid-breath, or in mid-sentence as I walk around talking to myself in this or that city, on this or that street in this or that land. All at once, fast as a shot, it's upon me, and all is darkness and dread.

I went to the pharmacy and got myself a bagful of tranquilizers. You can get them quite freely here, without a prescription, and my nightstand is covered with sedatives. Then I went to the store and got some liquor. I made two trips, as much as I could carry each time, and I'm strong. I just set the bottles on the stone floor and uncorked them. Then I lowered the Venetian blinds over all the windows in the small apartment, stripped completely, and went to bed. I took almost a handful of pills and swallowed them down with booze.

The mortal dread lodges *not* in my heart, but in my head—midway between my eyebrows, in my frontal lobes.

But it's also over there by the door, where the hangman stands waiting. Of course it isn't certain that he's standing. It's quite possible that he's sitting. Maybe he's seated himself on a chair over there. But I shall fool him, outwit the executioner.

Equipped with provisions—sleeping pills and alcohol—I can sleep myself away from him for hours at a time. Of course I wake up now and then, and he's still here in the dark room—with his faint, slightly snorting breath and the strange, rotten smell of cold around him. Then I curl up under the blanket, coil myself into the fetal position, wrap my feet in the bedclothes and feel the warmth of the bed all through my body. All is warm, soft, dark, and still. I lie on my left side so that my right arm is free for smoking and to fill my glass when it's empty. I can also help myself to the sedatives with it. Often I lie midway between sleep and waking, in a sort of half-dream in which all thoughts and memories turn into lightning pictures inside me. I see Ali's round face, the time I said to him: "Ali, how can a person sacrifice everything for a cause—for the revolution?"

"Jean," answered Ali, "have you ever saved a human life?"

"Yes," I replied; "strangely enough I have."

"What was it like?"

"Nothing special."

"Tell me exactly how it was, how it happened. But in the correct sequence!" he persisted.

"Well," I replied; "I'll try. In my fatherland, among the Eskimos, it's the custom to fasten wooden boards under one's feet and travel up and down the steepest snow-covered mountains. They call it 'walking on skis,' even if you don't actually walk. With these wooden things on my feet I was following a friend diagonally up a steep mountainside, straight through the snow, right at timberline. There we were, going along. Then I neither heard nor saw anything. I just noticed that something was happening, the air stood still around me, and the snow sifted down from the fine, thin birch branches. There was nothing but absolute silence. I continued in my friend's tracks for another couple of yards, and then the ski tracks ended as if they had been cut off with a knife. Two feet under the snow there was clean snow, but there were no tracks in it. Then I understood that there had been an avalanche. It had left a long trail up the side of the cliff, way up."

"And then?"

"Then I set out, following the trail. At the very bottom I found a few inches of ski pole protruding from the hard-packed snow. I pulled, but it didn't budge; that meant that he had the strap around his wrist. So I took off my skis and started digging down along the pole, then along his hand and arm, until I had uncovered his face. He lay there and laughed, and went on laughing long after I had dug him out. Then we went home to the ski lodge and got stinking drunk."

"And then?"

"There isn't any more," I said.

"Yes, there is," replied Ali: "What were you thinking about as you tracked him down and started digging?"

"About him."

"Could it have been dangerous for you?"

"I don't know—but I received the Carnegie medal of heroism: *Great it is to risk one's life to save another's!*"

"You didn't think about whether you were in danger?"

"I didn't have time."

"You asked me how a person can stake everything on a cause—on the revolution?"

"And you answered by asking me if I had ever saved a life."

"Exactly: You don't have time to think about anything else. You have only one thing on your mind."

I see much more inside me as I lie curled up under the blanket, full of sleeping pills and alcohol, feeling the soft warmth in my body and knowing that my consciousness is no longer made of barbed wire and pain. I see myself as a child, when I drank wine for the first time and knew that this, this was *my* drink . . . that it helped . . . assuaged . . . that it was living water . . . a magic potion. . . . Somewhat later, when I was ten, I drank up a whole cask of wine—ten gallons—while my parents were off on a trip. I had my first hallucinations then; I saw a lion sitting in my father's easy chair, a big, yellow, magnificent lion. And beside it sat a young man in a blue shirt and gray pants. The chair sagged under the weight of the lion. I felt no dread, either of the beast or of the man. On the contrary: my usual dread was gone, the blood no longer ran down the window frames and onto the floor, and all was soft and warm and still. The air between the boy and the lion and me was full of flowers and tendrils, and when I went to bed at night alone and drunk, then I wasn't afraid of the dark, and I no longer thought that the screeching of the cats outside in the wet autumn nights came from children being tortured. I lay as I'm lying now, with warmth and unconcern in my body, full of good pictures inside; I drew up my legs into the fetal position, just like now—and braided my arms, with my hands in my armpits or in my crotch, and all was softness and darkness and everything was good, but I knew that waking could be bad if I didn't set a jug of wine by the bedside. I didn't go to school, and I said to hell with all the schoolmates I was afraid of and the teachers I hated. I drank some wine as soon as I woke up, and all was well.

What happened then, I don't know. But afterwards there came a time of the usual sort, in which the darkness had returned and the schoolbooks were pasted together with blood, and I cried at night and dreamed of being chased out onto the pier by the mob and thrown into the black water, which was swimming with condoms and dead fish and slime. It didn't help to keep my hands in my crotch or my armpits; the cats in the cold, black garden were no longer cats, but mutilated children crying . . . all the same it passed, when I once again came across a goodly store of alcohol; I blossomed and lived like an ordinary child again. Only when that was gone did I experience something new: for the first time I drank up my father's shaving lotion, and he couldn't understand what had become of it.

All this is very near to me now, but it doesn't hurt anymore; I just know with a certain satisfaction, almost with joy, that it's always been like that, always the same sorrow, the same extreme insight into life. I feel it as if seen from the clouds, like a landscape far below me, something I've traveled through and can smile at. I lie curled up under the blanket, and I'm warm. Soon I doze off and can smile at everything. The warmth from my feet moves upward and fills my whole body, from the bottom up. My right arm is outside the covers, and in the darkness I grope for one of the boxes of sedatives, stick some pills in my mouth without swallowing, pick up the glass and find that it's empty, fill it again, and drink and swallow the tablets at the same time. I rejoice that I'm not asleep, because I've forgotten almost everything, and know that I will sleep soon, and that sleep is good and intimate. Ali's face smiles at me from the darkness, I laugh and mumble something. He wants to know if I've saved any more lives, and I laugh again and laugh and laugh. . . . I have an old gunshot wound and I laugh and the darkness is the best thing in the world.

When I wake up, I laugh at the executioner who sits over there by the door and smells bad. He's really ridiculous now, and all things coincide and the future is here and all that has happened is also around me, and the hangman has followed me stinking ever since I was a little child, and I am the stronger and I have my laughter on my side, I just laugh about Ali and me in the desert, I can hardly stop laughing at us, but before I think more closely about it or go on laughing, I'll have a couple of sleeping pills and a glass—and I take them and they don't stink the way the hangman is trying to do in order to paralyze me. Hardly anything really stinks if you just sniff it properly—if you really sniff, you'll find that garbage turns to roses, excrement to violets . . . oh God oh God . . . the last time we were in the desert, sitting side by side and looking down the long, flat road, straight as a taut bowstring, we saw a lonely African figure a long way ahead of us. Him we're going to stop for, said Ali, he can have a lift! As we approached the man, we saw how skinny he was under the ragged caftan which barely came down to the thin, bony knees above his bare feet and spindly calves. But most impressive of all was the way his head was poured into an enormous quantity of woolen blankets. Long before we had overtaken him, he stretched out his left arm and waved his slender hand. As he climbed into the back seat of the car, I saw that his front hair was spun into very thin strands of black and gleaming braids. I'd never seen that on an Arab before.

"Have a seat!" said Ali in French, without getting any response; so Ali repeated it in Arabic, but our passenger just shook his head amiably as he sat down and bent his head forward in prayer.

As Ali stepped on the gas, he gave me a sidelong glance and said: "Now you're seeing something! This man is no coastal Arab; he's so genuine that he not only doesn't understand French, he doesn't even understand a single word of Arabic. You're lucky to get to experience him!"

"Yes," I said.

"Most likely he only knows Berber," my black brother went on.

"Oh," I said.

"Maybe not even that," continued Ali.

"No," I said. I turned to look at our passenger as we drove on. I felt that life was beautiful and mysterious, and that we were all nameless wanderers, and so I sang loud and strong, in my best ballad voice:

"*Warum meide ich die Wege, die die andern Wandrer gehn. . .?*"

Our Arab passenger looked up and said in a high, bright, very nasal voice:

"*Ich bin aus München, meine Mutti ist Modekünstlerin.*"

"*Wo kommst' du her?*" said Ali without batting an eyelash.

"*Aus Baghdad,*" the Arab replied in falsetto: "*Schöne Stadt!*"

We chatted on with our passenger from Munich, and he told us with cheerful frankness how he had met a young Moroccan further north, and was now on his way to Marrakesh to see his beloved again. He had chosen to go on foot, like a pilgrim. That's what I call love.

Our little Arab was an honest and decent person, who took himself and the world as they were.

I lie in bed and all is darkness and peace around me; the sedatives and the alcohol have done their work. Him over by the door I don't worry about—he no longer frightens me now. All is just pictures and pictures, coming and going in a sort of half-sleep. Now and then it's a regular dream, and I suddenly feel blanketed by something paralyzing, like a great weight pressing on my chest, and I'm filled with terror because I know that not only is *he* in the room, but out in the bathroom there's another one, with horns and a tail. A frightful power streams from him, and I stiffen with dread. The evil majesty is no longer the way he was in Peretola, but a superhuman— even divine—being, with powers which are not of this world. I lie palsied with dread, but gradually something else makes its appearance, a rising indignation over his visit. And the indignation is because there are children in the house, and yet Satan has the monstrous impertinence, the gall, to show up in my bathroom. The indignation mounts to wrath, wrath to blind rage—and then I know what I'm going to do to him; I'll do the same to him as they do to bulls in the country, grab his tail and twist it. I know exactly how I'll take hold of his tail, I'll wrap it around my forearm so that I get a good grip, and then I'll twist it round. When I took hold, it seemed that my grip on his tail was successful, he whimpered and arched his back; but then he melted away between my fingers. When I woke up I was standing in the dark bathroom, groping for him. I turned on the light and looked around. I was alone.

Back in the darkness of the bed, I smiled to myself for a long time; I smoked and sipped at a drink until the pictures came back again.

I remembered another rescue, when an old friend of mine saved a life around ten years ago at a spa where she was staying. Even back then she was no longer young. One day she went down to the natatorium for a swim, and arrived to find herself all alone in the big room. As she swam out on the deep side, she thought she saw something below her, a very pale spot at the bottom of the green water; and as she swam on, it seemed to her that the spot had resembled the corpse of a child. But that was utterly impossible, and she brushed the thought away. Nevertheless, as she swam back she looked down through the water again, and the resemblance was still striking—so striking that she dived to the bottom to investigate. She came up with a naked, drowned little boy in her arms. After climbing out of the pool she emptied him of water, shaking him with his head downwards, and then breathed into his mouth. After awhile the boy started breathing by himself. He was the two-year-old son of one of the attendants at the spa; he had gone down to the pool for a bath. Sometimes the strangest things happen.

Afterwards she felt very happy that the boy was still alive.

Then there's something else, which keeps popping up. It happened thirty-eight years ago, and changed my whole life. I was fifteen years old at that time, and it was all because of a book. I read it through in one day; it wasn't that long. It was a thin book with contents of a descriptive sort; and even though I had been quite depressed in the previous fourteen years as well, still I can say that since reading this book I've never been happy again, or only for brief moments at a time. I've mentioned this before. I sat by an open window and read, and the book was called *The Concentration Camp Oranienburg* and was written by a man named Langhof, who himself had been a prisoner there, but who had later escaped abroad. There he wrote the book about Oranienburg, and it contained all the essentials about the concentration camps and the German treatment of prisoners. Things which made the civilized world gasp with horror and amazement after the war, I knew ten years earlier—from the time I was fifteen years old. It may be the most important book I've ever read, and it put an end to my childhood.

Many, many years later—it must have been around thirty years after that catastrophic summer day—I was in East Germany, sitting at the table in the actors' canteen in the basement of the theater which had been founded by my brother Brecht. Beside me sat a gray-haired old man, and we conversed about many things. When we got to the Teutonic

Golden Age in the thirties and forties, I told him the story of the book about Oranienburg. I remembered the author's name very well, and said that it was Langhof. The old man stared at me with a long, strangely puzzled look, then he said:

"I *am* Langhof."

The next time I got to Berlin, I brought along two bottles of Scotch for him. Langhof was dead. I drank them myself in his memory. It's good to have sedatives and liquor. From childhood until I was something over twenty years old I drank everything I could get my hands on. Then there followed a period of fourteen or fifteen years in which I never drank. That was while I was being initiated into the mysteries. Afterwards it was this world again, and I've been drinking ever since.

I can't survey all that alcohol has brought me into connection with, and I can't be thankful enough for it. When all is said and done, I know uncannily much about this world, and I've experienced many things. Most of them have happened in connection with alcohol. But I'm over half a century old, and I've seen enough now. I don't want to experience any more, I know the mysteries. The journey in the darkness is over.

The thought makes me so happy that I refill my glass; for some incomprehensible reason it was empty. With the liquor in my mouth I have to smile again—this time from joy that the journey through the night is ended. I shall escape seeing any more. I shall have an old man's peace in my soul. In my happiness I drink up quickly and fill the glass again. I become even happier because I don't need the accursed fluid any longer, it has done its duty by me. I say goodbye to it and thank it for a job well done. . . .Then I turn my back on it. Him by the door I've completely forgotten. I have to laugh when I think what I've experienced with the evil fluid. In particular I laugh about a time when I stopped drinking after an appallingly alcoholic period.

I had tried to stop several times, but relapsed after a day or two of relative abstinence. Each relapse was fiercer and deadlier than the last.

Then I woke up one morning and knew that it was over. I was right, this Sunday morning was a red-letter day. I drank nothing, but felt just fine. Then after awhile a slight shaking made its appearance, and presently I was shaking so much that I couldn't walk or stand or sit. Bed was the only possible place to be. I can't describe this shaking, for no one who hasn't experienced it would believe that it's true. But it wasn't exactly shaking, there simply isn't any word for it—yes, *tremens*. Then the air began to curl into small figures which were unpleasant to look at. One consolation, however, was music. Someone played for me, and it was the mightiest and most beautiful music I've ever heard. Then the doctor came with injections and medications. But I shook for four or five days in that incredible manner, although no, not all the time. That was that Sunday.

Funny that all this is past, I thought, and turned over on my side and drew my legs up into the fetal position. It was warm and soft, a perfect stillness. All was good.

Other memories glide through me. In one of the coastal towns of my childhood lived a Hebraic family. As far as I remember it consisted of the parents, two daughters, and seven sons. The youngest boy was my age, and we were equally black-haired and in the summertime our bodies were equally brown. The family didn't have an especially Jewish surname, but a Polish name which has nothing to do with the case. My friend was named Georg. We were always together in the summer at the beach, from the time we were twelve until we must have been around sixteen years old.

Georg was already a very accomplished trumpet player at fourteen, and at twenty a real musician. That fact played a decisive role in his life. Then for several years I didn't see any of that family. The next meeting I can date, for various reasons, in April 1943.

On that occasion we met in the apartment of a girlfriend of mine. The six elder brothers were there, but not Georg.

My girlfriend had an impressive talent for nymphomania, and being the only lady in the company, she had her plea-sures with each of us in turn. We had a great deal of booze on hand. Between copulations we talked. We talked all night. When we left the apartment, it had grown light outside.

What did we talk about?

For hours and hours the conversation consisted of my trying to talk them into getting out of the country and over to our eastern neighbor land, where no Teutons had any influence.

All the brothers refused in turn. They regarded me as hysterical, and they all assured me that so long as there hadn't been any announcement over the BBC, the Germans wouldn't try anything with the Norwegian Jews.

I explained to them that they were holding pogroms everywhere, and that our own country's turn would come very soon.

But again the same answer: Not until the announcement came from the BBC would there be any point in thinking about leaving.

I said that that was a misconception.

A few days later I myself went through the forest to Sweden.

The misconception had a result: Of the parents, two daughters, and seven sons, there was one who survived.

Many years passed, and one day at a party I was presented to a middle-aged man.

That man was Georg.

"We were all taken," he said; "we were waiting for word from London."

"How did you survive?"

"Played trumpet in the SS band."

As I lie curled up and warm and soft under the blanket, now sleeping, now waking—sometimes both at the same time—more shadows glide forth from the darkness of the past. One of them is Johannes who couldn't stand to be shut in. We shared a cell once, and he told me a great deal. I learned a lot from him. He suffered from the loveliest, most blooming claustrophobia I've ever seen, and he was almost always in prison. Once—to get out of solitary and over into the infirmary—he took a full box of matches and opened it halfway while he held it against his open eye. He set fire to the box and let it explode so that the blaze hit him right in the eyeball. It wasn't good, but it was better than solitary; he *got* to the infirmary. To escape from the cell he'd do anything, he ate everything from forks to the steel springs under his bunk. His whole belly, and his wrists and ankles as well, consisted of long, broad scars—Lord only knows how often he'd been slit open and basted together again.

One time he had been arrested in the magnificent county of Asker in my old fatherland, and the sheriff came into the cell to talk with him. During the conversation the sheriff put his glasses on the table—a pair of large, old-fashioned steel-rimmed spectacles; and when he left he forgot them.

A little later he returned.

"Have you seen my glasses?" he said.

"Yes," said Johannes.

"Where are they?"

Johannes pointed to his stomach.

"Does that mean that you've eaten them?" said the sheriff, in agitation, for it's always tiresome to lose one's glasses.

"Right," said Johannes; "I chewed them good first."

Again the infirmary. Again a new scar.

Much else goes through me as I lie in the darkness, feeling warmed through by pills and liquor—many, many things from half a century's life. There's no room for it anywhere.

Now and then I have to get up to make water; the drunkard's dark, stinking urine. All by myself I smell like a whole pissoir.

I see everything clearly, in a moment of white lucidity: Perhaps this is the moment of grace—or the moment of *dis*grace? It makes little difference. Everyone wants to be a prince, but nobody wants to pay the price. I know something about alcohol: Drunkenness is bound up with the structure and form of the entire personality, it's a part of the personality itself. I'm good for only two things: to keep my hellish records and to drink. That isn't just my picture of

myself—my *imago*; it *is* my personality. For almost twenty
years I've been like that. I've gotten used to it, and I can't
imagine myself any other way. If I am to stop drinking, not
only must the image of my personality be splintered and
destroyed, my personality itself must be crushed, pulver-
ized. This man who can't rest, who knows only hard work
or drinking like a madman, he must be annihilated. Then I
must build a new personality, starting at the very bottom.
Who can do that?

A while back I went into the old museum of handicrafts to
look at the beautiful antique vases. The guard had just finished
praying, the peace and dignity of prayer was still upon him.

"Were you talking with God?" I said.

"No," he said; "but I'm working to come closer to Allah,
I'm approaching Him inch by inch."

Again I take a fistful of sedatives, fill the tooth-glass with
cognac, and drink most of it down. Then I sleep for awhile. I
wake because I've wet the bed.

How many days I went on lying like this, I hadn't the
faintest idea. But I could feel with my hand that I'd grown a
beard. It ended with someone's ringing the doorbell. I let
them ring. Then they pounded. I let them pound. Then there
was a shout. It was Ali's voice. I sat up in bed and shouted
back. Then I got up, but I couldn't walk. Partly crawling,
partly leaning against the wall, I made my way to the door.
Once he was inside, he took me around the waist and helped
me; half carried me, back to bed. He looked around.

"If I drank the way you do, I'd die," he said.

"At least if you drank it all at once," I replied.

"I can't imagine it," he shook his head.

"You have no idea what a white man can drink," I went
on: "Not least in that sphere we're a superior race."

"Toward the end of their stay here the French drank like
lunatics. From morning till midnight. In the evenings they
were stinking drunk and would shoot at anything that
moved."

"Those must have been festive days."

I tried to light a cigarette, but couldn't manage to hold either it or the matches.

"Can you carry on a rational conversation?" he asked.

"No," I said, "but if you'll light a cigarette and stick it in my mouth every time I gape, and also find a bottle with something in it, I'll do my best."

He found an almost full bottle and poured some into my tooth glass. Then he lit a cigarette and sat on the edge of the bed, feeding me with it. He also held the glass up to my mouth.

"First tell me what day it is and what time of day!"

"It's almost two weeks since I've seen you," he said: "And it's morning."

"Fine, it's over now, I just don't dare stop too abruptly."

He looked at me for awhile.

"This is the last time we'll see each other."

"Is that true, Ali?"

He nodded, and I hadn't known how affected I would be at parting from him.

"They've shot at me again, this time in the morning when I was coming out the front door. It's only a question of days until they liquidate me."

I nodded.

"I'm not going back to the apartment again," he went on: "When I leave here, no one will know where I'm going. I have money and a new passport."

"To Europe?"

"Yes."

"It was good of you to come," I said, and took his hand.

"I didn't come just to say goodbye. I have to ask you a favor."

"Yes?"

He pointed to a briefcase which he had set on the floor.

"Will you go to headquarters with this?"

"Yes."

"Today?"

"I'll try. But I don't have the address." I was still holding his warm, soft hand.

He handed me a slip of paper. It contained the address
and the password.

"Give me a refill."

He went out to the kitchen and got a glass for himself.
Then we drank together, our final glass.

It was a rather rundown white villa, with a high white wall
around it and a green-painted iron gate. On the balcony a
black man stood playing catch with the Arab boys down in
the street. The house had probably been the residence of
some French official. I rang, and presently there was a voice
from within:

"Who are you?"

I responded with the password; then the door was
opened. Inside stood a young, athletic black.

"I've come from Ali," I said.

He gave me a warm and friendly smile:

"Welcome."

"I was supposed to deliver this to. . . ." I said.

He looked at the briefcase.

"Please come in. He'll be here in a moment."

I was led into a small room with two armchairs and an
Arabesque table.

"Coffee?"

"No thanks, but I'm in dire need of a big glass of brandy."

With a smile and a nod he went out. I felt better now than
in the morning, but I was shaking badly. He came back with
a tumbler of cognac, and I slowly drank it up.

I'm half a century old, and it feels like half a millennium.
The leader came in, and I rose to greet him, then I gave him
the briefcase from Ali.

"He went underground this morning," I said, "and I'm
supposed to give you his best."

He nodded:

"Come up to my office."

He was tall and very broad-shouldered, had a white cape over his shoulders and a fez on his head. That's how he looked, he whose dwelling-place nobody knew.

His office was big, furnished only with two easy chairs, a table like the one on the first floor, plus a large desk and a couple of bookcases. He set a bottle of cognac on the table and sat down in the other armchair.

I laid the slip with the address and the password on the table. Both must be forgotten.

"They'd begun to shoot at him on the street," I said.

He nodded.

We sat there for over two hours and talked. When the bottle was empty, I left.

Two days later I was down at Achmed's fish restaurant next to the mosque. I said goodbye to him. The meal lasted a long time; I ate fish soup first, and then scampi. After that, cheese, and finally fruit cocktail mixed with a generous quantity of anise. Then Achmed came running from the nearest coffee bar with the strong, hot coffee which you're never allowed to pay for. When I left, I took along some bread as always to get me past the flock of children, who were calmer today than usual. They know me and they know that they'll always get something without having to yell.

When I'd gone some distance past the flock, someone took me by the hand. It was the girl who had followed me up to the boulevard awhile back.

"*Bon soir*, monsieur," she said.

"*Bon soir.* How are you?"

We walked on for a bit in silence, and she squeezed my hand more tightly.

"Monsieur has been so nice to me."

"No," I said, "I wouldn't let you come home with me."

She nodded.

"Have you an appetite?" I asked.

"Yes!" she answered loudly.

We went into an Arab restaurant, and she was allowed to choose what she wanted to eat, and she chose rice with mutton. The waiter served the dirty little street urchin with the very greatest gravity and politeness. She ate like a wolf.

Afterwards she said:

"I've never met anyone who was as nice as monsieur."

Her black eyes glittered. And I thought how damned sad it was to be leaving this country. After the meal I drank up my last cup of coffee and went out onto the street with her. Again I took her by the hand.

"Adieu," I said: "Allah keep his hand on you."

She didn't reply, just looked at me with big eyes; in her hand she had five francs. Then she turned and walked down the street as before, with one hand clenched. Now and then she made a tiny hop and came down on the same foot.

That was my last evening in the country.

La Rue du Grand Peur

We revolutionaries are dead men on furlough.
Lenin

I walk slowly up the silver-gray street between the aged stinking houses which smell of turds and dishwater and children, cooking and old people. At its end a pair of naked treetops are silhouetted against the white sky. Autumn. I stop before a bar, go in, and drink an aperitif. Then I have another. I sniff at the smell in the bar for awhile, thank the proprietor and wish everything good to him and his family.

Outside I swing to the right and enter the Rue du Grand Peur, the Street of the Great Dread. A thin line of trees grows here; there are leaves still hanging on the branches. It's good for the soul to be in this lovely street again.

Some distance further down I meet Maximilien. As he was back then: at once elegant and virtuous, snobbish and ascetic. The first thing I look at is the big round scar along his lower jaw. The other scar is less visible.

Maximilien is not a tall man, and I have to think of the description which was given of him after the events of the tenth of Thermidor in the year 2: "The brute lived thirty-five years, was five feet two inches tall, had slightly compressed features and a sallow, bilious complexion."

I looked at him: the high, sloping forehead, the sharp nose, and the strong, jutting chin.

"Maximilien," I said; "now we'll drink a glass of wine.

Let's sit here."

We sat down at one of the tables on the sidewalk.

"Have you forgotten that I don't drink wine?" he said, and a gleam of virtue, of the saint, appeared in his eyes.

"No, no. Coffee?"

"Nothing."

We went into the restaurant, and I got my wine. He drank water. I thought how peculiar it was that this dandy, this snob, should have chosen temperance as his most distinctive trait.

"You never cared about women either."

"I had the people," he replied; "the good, honest, and decent people."

"Well," I said; "the people didn't turn out to be so good at the end."

"The people were misled."

We both sat in silence for awhile.

"What has happened?" he asked.

"There have been quite a few revolutions in this country since your time."

"How did they turn out?"

"The same as back then."

"The reactionary moderates, parvenus, and shopkeepers won?"

"All over again."

He brooded for a while, sunken into himself, and then he said:

"We were too lenient toward those who got rich on the revolution—the true enemies of the people."

"Lenin managed to bring it off," I said.

He looked up:

"Who is Lenine?"

"He who came after you. There's been a revolution in Russia too," I said; "and there they managed it: Lenin prevented the merchants and the moderates from taking over the nobility's wealth and privileges."

"You don't say. How did he do it?"

"Once the czar and the nobles had been crushed, Lenin

went on fighting against the moderates and crushed them too. In many things he built on your precepts. He too was a puritan by nature, ascetic and virtuous."

"Really?" Maximilien looked at me with big French eyes: "He succeeded?"

"He was a very witty man besides."

"Oh?"

"Not so witty as Vergniau, but very witty nonetheless."

When I mentioned Vergniau, Maximilien's old enemy, the corners of his mouth quivered. That's one of the few times I've seen the Incorruptible smile. Then he quoted:

"'Give Couthon a glass of blood, he's thirsty.'"

"There were many good speakers back then."

"Vergniau was the wittiest. But he was frivolous; he didn't know what morals were."

I sipped my wine calmly, looking at him.

"What did you mean by implying that this Le . . . Lenine—is that right?—built on some of my thoughts?"

"Just to mention one example: You said yourself that during a revolution every immorality, all depravity, all self-seeking is a counterrevolutionary crime and must be punished as such."

He nodded:

"That's what I said, and it's the truth: Virtue is the heart of the revolution. Only virtue, chastity, and selflessness can justify the dreadful price which the revolution exacts. Any egotism is a counterrevolutionary attack on the people."

"That's what Lenin thought too."

"He was right."

"Beyond that, Maximilien, I often think about you and about things you've said—in your speeches."

"Which ones?"

"Especially, perhaps, your speeches on the freedom of the press, the death penalty, the abolition of slavery, and the political rights of nonwhites—possibly most of all your last speech in the National Assembly."

"Do you really still remember them, Jean?"

"I know them by heart."

"Really?"

"I often think about the time you forced the National Assembly to endorse your declaration: *The French people recognize the existence of a Supreme Being and the immortality of the soul.*"

Maximilien was visibly moved.

"The feast day on Prairial 20th in the year 2 . . . I celebrated it. . . ."

"Maximilien, you lifted your hands heavenward before the altar of the Supreme Being, and you praised the Creator of nature, just as you likewise remembered and kept holy the Day of Chastity and the Day of Truth."

"I wanted to see a pure and modest, a virtuous, temperate people. I *loved* the people—and I was loved in return."

"In your last speech there's one sentence in particular which I often think about."

"Oh?"

"It's this: *I go, but I leave you this legacy: truth's terrors—and death.*"

Maximilien looked down:

"Did I really say that?"

"Exactly."

"Those are terrible words."

"The reality proved more terrible than the words. The great Thermidor began with you—*le grand peur.*"

"How was it with the other revolutions . . . did they also have their Thermidors?"

"All of them."

He poured himself another glass of water.

"But I don't just want to remind you of that line; you also said: 'What does it profit us to conquer the kings, when our vices conquer us . . . ?' And you said: 'My people, remember that freedom is but an empty word if justice does not reign supreme in the republic, and if the word "justice" does not mean love of equality and the fatherland. My people, you whom they fear, whom they flatter and despise, you the acknowledged sovereign whom they always treat as a slave, remember that where no justice is to be found, there the greed of officialdom shall reign; there the people have merely changed their fetters, but not their fate!' You also said: '. . . we must defend the people, even though we risk being called a despot; let scoundrels walk the road of crime to the scaffold—we shall walk the road of virtue!"

"That's right," he said; "during and after a revolution, righteousness—virtue—must reign absolutely."

"And this virtue, that was—the Incorruptible?"

"It was the people who gave me that name."

"The thought of absolute power in the right hands was another one which Lenin took from you, Maximilien."

"Hm."

"Do you remember your intervention in the National Assembly concerning the political rights of the blacks, the former slaves?"

He shook his head:

"I only remember that we got slavery abolished in all French colonies."

"That—your intervention—was in 1791. The planters on the Caribbean islands wanted the decree repealed, and aroused the sympathy of the business and farm interests in the National Assembly."

"Do *you* remember any of it?"

Maximilien spoke quietly, softly. A great calm lay over him.

"'Gentlemen,'" I quoted, "'I cannot forbear to refute an observation which has been presented here with the aim of belittling the freed blacks' interests. Remember that the question is not one of granting them their rights; remember that the question is not one of awarding them these rights; consider the fact that, on the contrary, the question is one of wresting from them rights which they have already been awarded. What man with any sense of justice could light-heartedly say to several million people: "We perceived that you had certain rights, and for that reason we regarded you as active citizens—*citoyens actifs*; but now we desire to plunge you back into misery and degradation; we wish to force you once again to your knees before the tyrannical masters whose yokes we helped you to cast off"?' (Here you were interrupted by applause at the very back of the hall by the extreme left wing.) You went on: 'But, we have been told, the question is a trifling one, of little consequence to the blacks; it concerns their political rights, we shall allow them to keep their civil rights.

"'But what then are civil rights, particularly in the colonies, without political rights? What then is a man in the colonies, when he has lost his rights as an active citizen and stands under the rule of the whites? He is a . . .'"

Here Maximilien interrupted me:

"Now I remember that speech . . . here we come to the main point!"

"'. . . a man who has neither direct nor indirect influence on the most important, most sacred requirements of the society to which he belongs; a man who is directed by officials whom he himself can have no part in choosing, a man who is eternally hampered by laws, ordinances, and administrative decisions. . . . He is a degraded man whose fate is subject to the whims, greed, and interests of a superior caste. These, then, are the benefits to which they ascribe a lesser significance!'"

Here the Incorruptible smiled again; he was content.

"Wait," I said: "You went on: 'It would not surprise me if they were to look with the same eyes on freedom, humanity's most sacred good, the sovereign value for every human being who stands apart from the beasts; it would not surprise me if, thinking in this fashion, they were to regard freedom as something superfluous, something the French people can nicely do without, if only they have bread and are left in peace. . . . But in my eyes, freedom remains a divinity; without freedom there is, for me, neither happiness, prosperity, nor virtue. . . .'"

"Did this Lenine build on my maxims on that point too?" said Maximilien.

"No."

"Then I can predict how it went."

"Freedom of the press?" I said: "Do you remember your

intervention about that?"

"That one I remember very well. It was one of the few speeches I learned by heart. I can still recite it."

He closed his eyes and spoke softly, every word as clear as ice:

"'Freedom of the press has always been regarded as the sole power which can oppose despotism, and it is therefore likewise natural that the principles upon which it rests should be blackened and perverted by despotic regimes—that is to say, nearly all regimes of whatsoever kind. Perhaps the very moment of revolution is a poor occasion on which to clarify these principles, for both sides still have painful memories of the wounds which the revolution has dealt; but we owe it to ourselves to rise above all prejudice and personal interest. . . .

"'Freedom of expression, which is truly the only road to liberty, must in no way be restrained or hampered, if we are not to find ourselves dealing with a despotic state.

"'But is it correct that liberty of the press consists only in the abolition of censorship and of all other restraints on its freedom? I do not think so—and neither do you, gentlemen. No freedom of the press exists so long as the author of a printed work can be subjected to arbitrary persecutions; and here we must draw a sharp line between criminal actions and so-called "crimes in print". . . . Where opinions are concerned, their criminality or their worth depends on their relation to the principles and ideas of reason, justice, and the public interest, along with a number of special circumstances; it follows that all questions of merit or criminality which may be raised in this connection must be left to all the uncertainty and caprice of individual judgment. Each will decide the question according to his own principles and ideas, his own personal interests; it is therefore understandable that a law concerning crimes in print can be adopted only after thorough going discussion . . . and it likewise becomes clear that such a law, passed under the pretext of safeguarding freedom of the press, almost inevitably has the effect of annihilating that freedom. Only think, gentlemen, of how it has been

hitherto, before the revolution—when the government persecuted writers in the name of public peace and order. Which
writings were made the object of public prosecution?
Precisely those which today are the objects of our admiration,
and whose authors today enjoy our homage. In truth, it lies in
the very nature of things that time and place should determine whether a writer shall be persecuted for his activities or
whether he shall be crowned with laurels. Three years ago
The Social Contract was incendiary filth. Jean-Jacques
Rousseau, the Revolution's greatest precursor, was an agita-
tor, a dangerous visionary; and had the government feared
the patriots' courage less, Rousseau had surely ended on the
scaffold; nay, one may add without fear of error: had the
despots trusted more in their own powers and in the people's
resignation to oppression, had the despots not feared a revolution—then Jean-Jacques Rousseau had surely paid with his
head for his services to truth and to humanity, lengthening
the illustrious list of those who in every age have fallen victim
to fanaticism, despotism, and tyranny. Now draw your own
conclusions, gentlemen; nothing is more subtle, yea nothing
more impossible, than to create a law imposing penalties for
the publication and expression of opinion concerning those
conditions which are the natural objects of human knowledge
and controversy. I for my part conclude that it cannot be
done. . . .'"

He finished abruptly and gravely.

We both sat silent for awhile.

"Still, your intervention concerning the death penalty
made the deepest impression," I said: "That was at the end of
May, 1791."

Maximilien turned his head toward the window, so that I
saw his sharp, imposing profile against the light.

"I remember that, now that *you* remind me of it, Jean."

Without turning his face from the window he continued
solemnly:

"'Scarcely had the news reached Argos that the Athenians
had doomed its citizens to death, before the people hastened

to the temples and implored the gods to turn the citizens of Athens from their cruel designs. I come to entreat not the gods, but you, the lawgivers who are their interpreters and spokesmen, to strike these bloody laws from the statute books of France. . . .'"

He fell silent and turned his face to me. I continued:

"'Has society the right to impose a death penalty? The question can be answered in a word: Society has no other prerogative than that which is given to every human being; namely, the right to redress of grievances. But if the recognition of this right—even independent of the body politic—entails definite limits, set by reason and nature, which forbid any person to demand exaggerated redress or to take a cruel revenge, can that person then kill his enemy? Yes—but in one case only: namely, when this frightful deed is done out of pure self-defense. Now apply the spirit of this principle to society; the people have said: Our individual powers are too weak to protect our peace and our rights, now let us join forces to create a public power which will transcend the strength of sundry individuals, let us unite our several wills into a common will which in the name of law shall sanction and fix the rights of each; let us pass sentence on all who presume to violate these rights. Thus did lawful punishment supplant the individual's natural means for averting and punishing wrong. But if, now, the right degree of harshness to be used against an enemy depends on the avenger's might, then there can be no doubt but that society is obliged to exercise far greater lenience than a man who must prosecute an injustice alone!'"

Outside, the sky of early afternoon stretched over the Rue du Grand Peur and over Paris; the dull silvery light flowed in over us, it glittered in the water carafe and sparkled in the wine.

Now Maximilien softly took up the thread from me:

"'I have said to you: before the social contract—before the formation of the body politic—a man had the right to kill his enemy only when this somber deed took place out of pure necessity. But can this exceptional situation ever obtain with respect to a whole society's power over a single culprit? We need only illumine this one point, and the death penalty is doomed. If, outside the society, an enemy comes and threatens my life, or if after being chased away twenty times he returns yet again and destroys the field which I have planted—then I have only my own strength to pit against his; I must go under or kill him, the natural law approves and justifies my action. But if—within the society—the common might is directed against a single individual, by what principle of justice would they then be justified in killing him? And let particular stress be laid on one crucial circumstance: If the state punishes a culprit, he can then no longer harm the society; it puts him in chains, it can condemn him unimpeded, society can render him harmless—with all the means which untrammeled authority has at its disposal. A conqueror who slaughters his prisoners, him we call a barbarian. An adult who murders an erring child instead of teaching it, him we call a monster. . . .'"

"Here," I said, "you were interrupted by wild yells of rage from the moderates and conservatives, and Abbé Maury stood up and roared in a fury that you could go peddle your maxims in the Bois de Bondy!"

Maximilien smiled gently at the memory. He then pursued the train of thought further:

"'It is thus established, all prejudice notwithstanding, that the scenes of horror which society arranges with such great splendor are, in the eyes of morality and justice, nothing else than ritual national murders.'"

Maximilien paused for a moment, considered and went on—now approaching the end of the speech:

"'Furthermore, gentlemen, why will you doom yourselves never more to extend a hand to one who is wrongly convicted? These vain confessions of regret, this hypocritical rehabilitation of the dead, a rehabilitation which you bestow on the lifeless shadow, the insentient ash, is a very feeble means by which to make amends; it is but a sorry proof of the

criminal law's barbaric insolence. Only to Him whose ever-
lasting eyes see into the depths of our hearts, only to Him
does it fall to pronounce an irrevocable judgment. You, the
lawgivers, cannot take upon yourselves this dreadful office
but by cumbering yourselves with the innocent blood which
the sword of the law has shed.

"'Beware of obscuring the relation between true punishment and exaggerated harshness; the two are opposites. Just
and temperate laws will be accepted by all; but against cruel
laws all will conspire. Aversion to the crime will be counter-
balanced by the sympathy which arises at the thought of an
overharsh punishment. . . . Every person will faithfully
deliver up the culprit if the punishment be mild, but the
thought of sending a man into death sets his human nature
atremble within him. Yes, I say to you without hesitation:
The lawful duty to denounce the guilty one, the duty which
you have enjoined on all citizens, is intolerable, absurd, and
incapable of fulfillment if you let the death penalty stand. . . .

"'That the happiness of society is *not* bound to the death
penalty, is indubitable. . . . And neither is there any doubt but
that the tender, sensitive, freedom-loving people of France—
whose virtues are now to ripen under the rule of liberty—
wish to treat the guilty in a humane fashion; and it is beyond
all doubt that experience and wisdom will lead you too, gentlemen, to those principles which comprise the core of my
intervention—namely, to abolish the death penalty!'"

He bowed his head and was silent.

"As a reward for that, you reaped hatred."

"From all the moderates and from those who were getting
rich on the revolution. Not from the people. They loved me.
They called me 'The Incorruptible'."

"The National Assembly went against you."

"A small handful from the extreme left went along. Sade
was the only one who really supported me on the death
penalty. He also supported me on the blacks' political rights."

"The marquis?"

"The old marquis."

"Donatien-Alphonse-François de Sade?"

"Right. He formulated the question as none of the others could: *You let a person die, honored gentlemen, because he has killed another. Then there will be two dead instead of one.*"

"The marquis was a libertine, sensual, lewd," I said.

"In his youth. When he unleashed the storm on the Bastille, he had been in prison under the old regime, without due process of law, for thirteen years. He was a chastened man, a true revolutionary. On the twelfth of July he called down from his cell window to the crowd that the prisoners were being maltreated, and that the Bastille must be stormed and freedom and justice brought into the land. Two days later the people smashed the gates and freed the prisoners, but some time passed before we found Sade, who had been transferred from the prison to the security ward in the Asylum of Charenton. During the revolution he was a brave, virtuous soldier, he performed faithful service in the Eighth Company of the *Section des Piques* and as a commissar for the cavalry. Sade wasn't lewd, he was a political *citoyen actif,* a man of soul, even though he was trained as an officer and at fifteen was already a lieutenant in the Royal Infantry Regiment. No, he wasn't vicious, he wrote the truth about the vices of the nobility and the powerful. He described—as he said himself—a depraved century. He was a courageous man and an honest one—a very honest man."

"After the revolution he was locked up again for another thirteen years, until his death. That makes a total of twenty-six years without due process of law," I said.

"I'm not surprised."

"It was the little butcher from Corsica, Napoleon, who kept him inside."

"Napoleon?"

"Bonaparte."

"Never heard of him. Don't want to hear about him either."

"So you and Sade fought together for lenience and humanity?"

"We two."

"You've both gone down in history as the bloodiest of the bloody."

"That's quite natural."

"The story bulges with executions and terror."

"We practiced no terror. You all forget that it was in self-defense; we were at *war!* The king's lackeys were marching into France along with the Germans, with an enemy power. The young republic was fighting for its life, the fatherland faced the gravest peril; those who worked for the royalists and the Germans were traitors to the fatherland, traitors to freedom—and they were executed with good reason. When a monarchy executes people, nobody says a word. Because we republicans and revolutionaries, we were at once proclaimed to the whole world as bloodhounds and murderers. . . . No, we conducted no terror. France was defending her life against enemies from without and within—we were in extremis and acted from necessity."

We sat silent for awhile. I said:

"I know nothing about your childhood and youth?"

"I had no childhood, I had no youth."

"I mean it only in the literal sense, the earliest years of your life; you were born in '58—the same year that Damien was executed."

"A year and a half after the long, loathsome vivisection of an execution which Louis XV had them carry out in public. When I was yet a small child I heard all the particulars. I remember every detail to this very day—among other things they poured molten lead into the wounds left by the torture, and burned off one of his hands. Half the nobility of France stood in the windows and watched, drinking toasts and feeling each other's sex organs—citizen Sade described it."

"Is that the kind of thing you're thinking of when you say that you never had a childhood?"

"No. I became the head of the family when I was six years old."

"Is that possible?"

"My mother was a good, loving woman—seduced, but a chaste and virtuous mother. She passed away when I was six years old, and I was the eldest—my father was a rake and an immoral man, he deserted us again and fled the country. I ended up as both mother and father to my siblings, Charlotte-Henriette and Augustin."

"He left you all three in the lurch?"

"Exactly."

"What did you live on?"

"The mercy of relatives. Genteel begging—charity, alms. I saw to it that the children were brought up as virtuous, decent people."

The Incorruptible raised his head with its strong cheekbones and looked at me with large, French eyes.

"What was your father?" I asked.

"Like everyone in the family he was a lawyer, one of the thousands of shifty pettifoggers who swarmed over France and sucked it dry. He fled his responsibility for his children, and became a language teacher in Germany. Frivolous and unprincipled, without honor, but clever. He also dishonored my mother, got her pregnant, so that she was forced into the marriage. I was born four months after the wedding."

"What were your school days like, Maximilien?"

"First there was the schooling in Arras, with only priests as teachers; later—when I was eleven years old—I came to the College Louis-le-Grand in Paris."

"What sort of a pupil were you?"

"My sole concern was to show that philanthropy wasn't wasted on me. I read."

"Had you no free time?"

"I must have had some."

"What did you do then?"

"I remember that I was fond of raising pigeons and sparrows. Once I gave a pigeon to my sister, but she didn't look after it conscientiously enough, so one stormy night it got left out in the garden, and there it died."

"Your siblings also got schooling."

"My sister went to a school for poor girls."

"Your brother?"

"Received the same education as I did. I supported him while he was a student."

"When did you finish at the university?"

"When I was twenty-three years old I got a licentiate from the University of Paris. I went home to Arras and became a lawyer."

"You were a judge as well?"

"A year later I became a judge, and was also elected to the Academy in Arras."

"Maximilien, have you ever pronounced a death sentence?"

He paused before answering:

"Yes."

"What was it like?"

"I broke down completely and stayed in bed for several days. At that time my sister was living in my household, and she nursed me devotedly."

"Politics?"

"In '88 I published my *Appeal to the Nation of Arras.*"

"Maximilien, may I ask you something?"

"Yes?"

"Citizen Robespierre," I said; "what was it like to die?"

"Death is the beginning of deathlessness."

"What do you mean?"

"I don't believe in the necessity of life, only in virtue and Providence."

"It's true all the same that you terrorized France," I said: "Not with your cruelty, but with your virtue."

"Terrorized?"

The round eyes became even bigger than usual.

"It isn't easy to put up with a person who is referred to all over France as 'the Incorruptible'."

"I see."

"But what was it like to die?"

He thought about it:

"It was right."

"What do you mean?"

"I knew early that I would not dwell long among you."

"The moment of death itself?"

"That I hardly remember. I just know vaguely that I was brought to the scaffold amid the roars of the duped, misled people. During my arrest I was hit by a pistol shot which smashed my jaw. Then they laid me on a table with a wooden box under my neck. A cretin of a doctor came to look at me; he rooted around in my wounds with his probe and then pulled some of my teeth. All I could think about was that the guards mustn't hear me groan. The pain was so intense that the last twenty-four hours before the guillotining was only a bloody mist. But they never heard me complain. They tied a bandage around my head to support my lower jaw. I was conscious the whole time; I didn't sleep. When they took me to the scaffold, it was in an old cart with no springs; every movement, every bump from the pavement was unbearable. The blood ran down over my collar and clothes. When I was laid on the board, the executioner tore off my bandage with a violent wrench. That was the one time I screamed. When they tipped the board, my jaw came into contact with the half-moon indentation on the block—*la lunette*—where the neck is supposed to lie. But I didn't make a sound."

"Your brother was executed the same day as you?"

"The same day."

Chapter 5

Among my papers lie a bundle of yellowed sheets which I wrote as a young man:

In Alexandria there lived a youth who converted to the Christian faith. After the baptism he felt a great lack, and he went to his teacher and said: "I believe that great pain and suffering are to be found on the earth, and I know them not; therefore I wish to go out into the world to learn to know all suffering and all pain. Until I comprehend all the evil which happens, I cannot begin a life in truth. All that I feel, think, and say will be a lie, so long as I do not know all the pain in the world."

His teacher, who had instructed him in the faith and in the mysteries, looked at him and said:

"My son, in this as in all else which touches your heart, you yourself must choose. And what you say is correct; no one can live in truth until he knows evil. Still I would warn you: the journey upon which you are embarking may become more dangerous than you know. You are young, you are unsettled in the faith, and the truth can be a heavier burden than you have shoulders to bear. Rather remain here, immerse yourself in study, live in piety and labor; do not seek out suffering."

The youth replied:

"My father, this has come over me as that which is stronger than a thought. I must go forth to acquaint myself with evil."

"I shall pray that the angels of the Lord may follow you," answered the teacher; "you know not what you do."

The youth bade farewell to family and friends, took a staff in his hand, and went forth. The journey proved to be very long.

After a few hours' wandering, his way led him along the edge of a desert. Here the youth left the road, went apart into the desert, and fasted for three days and nights. Then he made a vow: Never to think of himself and his own life, never to lose sight of the truth about others' sufferings, always to feel the pain of others as his own.

Afterwards he offered up a prayer:

"Lord, Maker of the earth and of the universe, Thou who didst create the stars and the night and the sea and the wind and the mountains, Thou who didst create the sun and all the living things of water, earth, and air! Thou hast created me, who am no more than a worm—acquaint me with all the world's pain, let me feel all the world's sorrow, let me never forget the evil I have seen!"

When he turned, a desert hare was sitting behind him, and he understood that the Lord had granted his prayer. Then he rose and departed. But he passed a man of God who dwelt alone in the desert, and the man called after him, and the youth turned back and knelt before him and said:

"Speak, your son listens."

And the hermit replied:

"I see by your face that God has set his mark on you. Have you a wish?"

The youth was moved and said:

"I would learn to know all the world's evil and all pain, to the very bottom would I know it, that I may live in truth and not in falsehood."

"Will you also learn to know the greatest pain?" said the hermit.

"Yes," replied the youth; "the greatest."

"You know not what you say, but your wish shall be fulfilled. The day it is accomplished, you shall remember me and think on what I say: See you the plant which stands by the spring?"

"I see it."

"It would not live a day, did the angels of the Lord not sustain it. Will you remember that?"

"I shall remember."

The youth returned to the road, and after a time he found a dog lying by the wayside. The people had left it to lie there, for it was sick and could no longer keep up with the beasts and with those who had gone on. It was in great pain and moved its head back and forth, and it did not understand why it was in such pain. And it whimpered. The youth took up a stone in order to kill it, but he was not used to killing, so that he struck several times, first on one side of its head, then on the other, and the dog tried to creep away from him as he struck, but could not. At last it lay still and whimpered no more. The youth went on, but his hands trembled, for it was the first time that he had killed.

In his childhood he had been spared many things.

He journeyed on and came to great cities, and he saw all the pains of humanity, he saw the pain of mothers as they gave birth, and he saw the pain of mothers over their dead children. He saw children sold as slaves to the glassworks, where they could live no more than a few years because of the heat from the kilns. He saw these children sleep in chains at night, he saw them cease to grow, he saw death become visible in their faces. He saw the pain of men in war, and of prisoners when they were put in irons, or when they were blinded. He saw people flayed as a punishment for disobedience, or torn to bits with tongs. He saw the pain of the lonely, the forsaken, the outcast—and he was ashamed at all the pain and injustice which did not befall himself. He thought that all the world was like a woman in travail, and that only with the greatest pain could the new humanity be born. This faith did he have.

He had yet much to see, it took him many years, and when the day came when he had seen all the pain in the world, he was no longer a youth, but a man with furrows in his face, and all that he had seen lay like glowing coals within him. He burned with sorrow over all that he had learned to know. But he said to himself:

"Now you have seen all pain, you have seen that the world is a woman in travail who shall give birth to the new, higher being. Go out into the desert and speak to God; perhaps He will answer you, so that you may begin a life in truth, for now you have seen the truth."

When he turned his back upon men, he was seized at once with a strong disquiet over what was now happening in the cities, and whether new sufferings and pain had not come to the people. For that which he had seen he could not forget, nor could he stop thinking of what the people were now doing to one another, for he knew that their hearts were very hard. He turned and went back to the city.

There he saw that the people treated one another as before, but more harshly; the evil in the world increased like the summer swarms of flies around a dead beast. And he saw that the new being was not aborning, but that each pain begot a thousand new pains, and that every wrong begot new wrong, and that the evil among men was stronger than the good. And each time an evil came to pass, he observed it closely and saw that it created new evil, and he saw that guilt lay over the earth like a black cloud, and that it blotted out the sun. Now he saw straight into the human breast, and saw that none could forget the evil and the injustice which had been dealt them, and that their hearts grew ever harder.

In the marketplace of the city he cried out to God:

"Show me a person who can forget the pain and the injustice which he has had to bear, show me just one!"

God did not answer him, and the man thought that in this way the new being would never be born. His heart was almost breaking, and he thought: When I cannot forgive the wrong which befalls *others*, how then can I expect that others should forgive that which befalls *themselves*?

He looked around him in the world and saw that all was pain, and that suffering was without end. He wept.

The next day he sought new pains and new injustice on earth, and he felt that now he saw more rightly and more truly, for he no longer believed that the world was a woman in travail, and he no longer believed that the new being would be born through pain. He saw that the evil came not from human nature, but from the way in which people lived together on earth, and that this way was evil and lacking in righteousness—but it was a crux to his thought that even this way of living together, this too had come from men's interior, they themselves had created it, the strong and the mighty had created it out of their own evil lust after power.

Day after day he saw new sufferings, and he had wholly lost the ability to forget any of the evil which he had seen. At night not even sleep could bring oblivion; he cried out from evil dreams.

He shouted to God:

"What have I done, that I should have this insight: That suffering is without end!"

God did not answer.

Again he went out into the desert to find solitude and to speak to the Lord, but when he had been walking for half a day, he felt that he was fleeing from the sight of the sufferings which visited humankind, and he turned and said:

"Never shall I flee from that which happens on the earth!"

Again he saw new pains. He went to the places of execution and saw people's eyes put out and their bowels torn to bits, and he said to God:

"Why hast thou created life on earth thus? Why hast Thou created us thus, that we do these things against each other? Why hast Thou so created us, that the strong act unjustly toward the weak?"

Now came the day when he no longer wished to go out into the desert. He understood that he could no longer leave

what he saw, but that he was bound to it, and that he had no
eyes for anything save suffering and guilt. All else appeared
to him like a dream or a mirage. If he saw a child play and
laugh, at the same time he saw within himself all the suffering
he had seen in his life; then he no longer saw the child smiling in play, he saw it bowed with tears over pain to come.
Then he understood that the wish of his youth was accomplished; he knew that he had seen all the world's pain and
that he would never forget it. Now he himself belonged to
that which he had seen.

He cried to God:

"Lord, I have seen all the earth's pain, I bear the whole
world's sorrow! I can forgive nothing! I am like a dead dog
by the wayside. Let now Thy servant be freed of his life! A
life in truth I cannot bear!"

The Lord did not answer. He cried anew:

"Why dost Thou let the people founder in their own
wickedness? Are there no bounds set to their deeds?"

He turned his back to the Lord and went among the people and saw that no limits were set to their actions. Each had
full freedom to do all the evil he would, and to the wickedness of kings and of the mighty there were no bounds whatsoever. He saw warriors tear out the tongues of the conquered, make them into slaves, cut up pregnant women with
knives and spit the unborn on their lances, and never did the
angels of the Lord intervene and put a stop to their acts.
Then he said to himself:

"I was right. Suffering has no end. The people are like
mad wolves against one another, the pain is without cease. Of
all things on earth, death is the only good."

And he cried to the Lord:

"Now let me die!"

He cast himself on the ground and foamed at the mouth,
and he shrieked like one possessed:

"Let me forget! The pain which I now have within me is
greater than all the pains I have seen, for I bear them all
within me!"

The Lord gave him no oblivion. And he went out into the desert and lived like a wild beast. He fasted and scourged himself with thorny branches and scraped off his skin with sharp stones, but he forgot nothing, not a whit did he forget of that which he had seen. He sat down in the desert and cried out, and the wild beasts shunned him. He howled to the Lord like a wolf, saying:

"Let me forget!"

He rolled in the sand, but he received no forgetfulness. Then he shrieked to God:

"I spoke to Thee when I was a child and knew not what I asked—is Thy heart just as hard as the people's?"

He was as one possessed, his hair and beard and nails were never cut, and he was naked in the wilderness. Burning coals lay in his breast from all that he had seen. He wept. He said to himself:

"Can any pain be greater than the knowledge of good and evil?"

One morning he sank into deep thought, so that he thought all the day, ever asking himself:

"Could it be that any pains were greater than this? Could it be that I have not yet met the greatest pain?"

After three days he arose and went among the people to seek the final pain. When he met the people again, he thought: Who am I that I would chastise them?

He was like a beast to look upon, with burning eyes, and they cast stones and dung after him, and he paid them no heed, but he understood them. He went to the temple of Moloch and the temple of Baal, where the priests were placing children in the idols' glowing hands, as they cried:

"Verily Baal-Zebub is great! Verily Moloch is mighty!"

He heard the dying screams of the children, and he said to himself:

"This pain is frightful, but the suffering of the innocent children is no greater than that of the sinners."

He called to the Lord:

"Lord, why dost Thou not overturn with Thy left hand

this whole abomination of a world?"

The Lord did not answer. He cried louder:

"Is it then all the same which god one cries to? Can none answer?"

All the pain and all the evil which he had seen now rose up in him, and he said to himself:

"There is no God, and all this pain is without meaning. Never will the lamentations of humanity reach the ear of any god. Everything under the sky is meaningless, and the new being will never arise." He wept but he did not cry out, and he went back into the desert and lived in a cave.

There he spoke to the beasts of prey and the vultures and the scorpions and snakes of the desert and taught them, saying:

"There are no limits to evil. Suffering is without end. Pain has no meaning."

And the jackals and the hyenas and the carrion vultures, the scorpions and the snakes answered him:

"Truly you are right! All is meaningless!"

"The scales are fallen from my eyes," he said to himself: "Now I live in truth. I bear the final pain, but I live. I am still alive. Now I shall go among the people and be as one of them, for I will no longer bear all the world's guilt, but only my own; yet I wish to be among them and help them. All pain is without meaning."

He could not stand on his feet for sorrow, for he was still filled with the lamentations of all humanity, and they were like a boulder to bear. On hands and knees he crept to the spring, for he thirsted, but he lay prostrate by the spring, having no power to drink, and he thought: This is death, blessed be thy coming! And he laughed aloud. Then he said to himself:

"Today I have laughed like a young man!"

He fell into a long swoon, and when he woke, he drank of the spring, and he saw that beside it stood a young plant, as fresh as if the rain had fallen upon it. Then he remembered a man of God whom in youth he had promised to remember on the day when he had seen the greatest pain. He said to himself:

"Truly in this spring and in this plant there is no sin."
Then he cried so loudly that all the angels heard him:
"Praised be the glory! I have seen the flowing water and the green plant!"
The next day he went to the city of his birth. His eyes were like the eyes of an old man. But his teacher still lived, and was advanced in years.
"My son, have you seen all the world's pain?" said the sage.
"All," replied the man.
"Even the last one?"
"The last."
Then the Lord has spoken to you, since you stand before me now."
"I saw a spring of flowing water and a green plant."
"Then let me see if you can smile," said the sage.
And the man smiled, almost like a youth.

I'm back in the courtroom where I belong—among the insulted and the injured and the weak, among the helpless, the hopeless, and the abused, among the wrongly convicted and the justly convicted. I look at them and I listen to them. Yes, I've come home. I have no duties, I don't put carbide in the inkwells, nor urinate in the bloody sawdust on the floor.

But I have understood the trial's higher meaning—its ideal truth, so to speak: that injustice can be turned into justice. When the hour of upheaval comes.

For what else is the revolution but the absolute court case? The revolution is the last and highest and most terrible form of reckoning. Now the executioners stand as the accused; the oppressed, the degraded, the wretched sit as accusers, judges, and jury on the case. It won't prevent new injustice, but this time the wrongs are on the other side—in other words: even though the revolution entails guilt, yet the guilt is part of the justice. I remember a king who said, *Après nous le déluge.* Well, it came. When the Marquis de Sade, one lovely day in July, cried to the people that they must storm the Bastille, the tidal wave soon followed, and it didn't inquire who was just or unjust. The same goes for the Flood in the Old Testament: it didn't ask either; it merely saved a male and a female of every species. I can't imagine that all the doves, lions, and lambs who didn't get onto the Ark were guilty of mortal sin. Many of the executed creatures were surely both kind and good.

Nonetheless: the men of the Revolution wanted to create justice, and justice is terrible—but blessed are they who hunger and thirst after righteousness. Even though the best thing would be for God to forgive us our trespasses, as we forgive those who trespass against us.

I've kept my concluding records, for twenty-one years I have kept them, and that's quite a piece of a man's life; I began with the Teutons' medical experiments on living people. It was my task to keep the court records. They may have a meaning or they may not. But I've learned something from them.

All that happens is necessary—it may not have *been* necessary, but it has *become* necessary. And that the revolution is coming in the way that it *must* come, *that* would not have been necessary either, had *we* not made it so.

I write this during the great silence, the silence before the hurricane.

One of the wrongly convicted lately said to me: "Now think no more about injustice and evil, but create a new world where all shall love each other."

I don't believe that humanity is evil, nor that humanity is good—I believe that a human being is partly evil and partly good. Which side shall be permitted to grow and develop depends on ourselves. On a planet where people have freely chosen to let themselves be burned alive for the sake of truth, the good must have great possibilities. The court sat, the charges were read, the witnesses heard, the evidence presented; humanity was found guilty. I kept the trial records.

But I miss one voice in the courtroom: that of the defense.

His plea will be a song of praise—of man the incomprehensible—endlessly evil, endlessly good—all-renewing, all-destroying.

And so the journey is ended, Columbus.